THE NOBODY MAN

THE NOBODY MAN

THE AARON HOLT SERIES
BOOK 1

MIKE RYAN

Copyright © 2024 by Mike Ryan

All rights reserved.

No part of this book may be reproduced in any form or by any electronic or mechanical means, including information storage and retrieval systems, without written permission from the author, except for the use of brief quotations in a book review.

Cover by The Cover Collection

1

They called him The Nobody Man. He was a shadow, a figure that could effortlessly blend into the background of just about any situation. No one knew his real name, or where he came from. No one other than his CIA contacts, that is. But his enemies knew the nickname. Usually after he had already gone. If they weren't dead.

But even hearing that The Nobody Man was near was enough to send many criminals into hiding, going so deep that they thought no one could touch them. Of course, that wasn't true. If he was after them, there was nowhere deep enough that they could hide.

And sometimes, it was just their own paranoia getting the best of them. Hearing a whisper that The Nobody Man was near, whether it was actually true or not, made many men and women sweat themselves into a panic attack. The Nobody Man navigated through life like a ghost, leaving behind a faint trace of his existence.

His real name was Aaron Holt. His appearance was as unremarkable as his presence. He had an average build, medium height, and plain features that could easily fade into a crowd. He wasn't thin or overly muscular. He wasn't ugly, but didn't have movie-star looks, either. He was just your plain, average, everyday-looking kind of guy. And he used that to his advantage.

Beneath Holt's outer layer of extreme plainness lay an extraordinary ability. The Nobody Man possessed an unmatched talent for blending seamlessly into any environment or situation. He had perfected the art of adapting to his surroundings, becoming anyone and everyone he needed to be. From high-profile corporate events to gritty back-alley dealings, Holt effortlessly slipped into any role he chose. His chameleon-like ability allowed him to gather intelligence when it was needed, or to eliminate a target when it was necessary.

He first acquired the nickname due to the frequent questions that came after his assignments. Due to the secretive nature of most of his missions, whenever someone asked about what happened, or who did it, the response from his superiors was usually the same.

"It was nobody."

It became such a frequent response that most people in the organization didn't even know his real name. He just became The Nobody Man. It was also a good name to use when someone asked a question that they really didn't want the answer to, such as being involved in an assassination that surely would have brought major questions from around the globe.

"Were we really involved in that?" someone would ask.

"Not us," would be an often reply. "It was nobody that we know."

Even in his private life, he'd grown accustomed to living in the shadows. He loved the quiet life. He embraced it. Probably because of all the assignments he had in the CIA. They were usually anything but quiet. Or dull.

But it'd been three years since his last assignment. There'd been overtures, of course, by some of his former associates. And by some people he'd never even met before. All of whom had hoped to entice him back into the life which he only gave up to be with his sick wife, Denise. But his answer was always the same.

"Not now."

Not while his wife still needed him. Denise had fought for the last three years to get rid of the terminal disease which had overtaken her. The last few months had been the worst. She was bound to a wheelchair now, not able to stand for even five seconds without her legs giving out. Her diagnosis was that she had five or six months left. If she was lucky.

That diagnosis was given about two months ago. That's why they tried to cherish every second they had left. Together. They'd been an item for about twelve years, married for eight, first meeting in high school. And they stayed together ever since. She understood about the secretive nature of his work, and his occasionally flying off at a moment's notice, usually halfway around the world. She never asked him about it, though. And when he was gone, she threw herself into her work as a divorce attorney.

Denise was also what grounded him when Holt returned. She was what kept him from flying off the deep end. She kept him humble. She kept him sane. When he was back with her, all the unimaginable and unthinkable things he had to do... they just drifted away. As if someone else had done them.

They lived on a large property on a lake, with nothing but acres of trees around them. One of their favorite activities now was just sitting by the edge of the lake, watching the water, and the ducks as they swam by.

At this moment, Denise was already by the lake, waiting for her husband to join her. Holt, though, also had to take care of their aging fifteen-year-old American Bulldog. Brutus was Holt's Christmas present from his parents as a teenager. Now, though, tumors riddled his body, and his legs had given out on him, unable sometimes to even go outside to use the bathroom.

Holt had just picked up his eighty-pound friend and put him outside, as he often had to do. After a quick bathroom trip, Brutus plopped down again, as he often did. Holt picked him up and brought him down to the lake, putting him between Denise and himself. They both took turns petting him. He also liked to watch the ducks swim by.

"It's not going to be the same without him," Denise said.

Holt lowered his face and kissed Brutus on the top of his head. He fought back tears, knowing this would be the last day he had with him. Holt was sad, unsure if he was doing the right thing by putting his dog down tomorrow. But he didn't want Brutus to suffer. And while Holt didn't mind cleaning Brutus off after his frequent accidents, he knew it was time to let go, regardless of how hard it was.

The three of them sat there for a while, silently, just watching the water. It looked so peaceful. It was almost enough to make them forget about all of their current troubles. Almost.

"Aaron, we've been putting this conversation off for a while."

Holt sighed, having a feeling he knew what was coming. "Dee, I really don't want to—"

Denise took his hand. "Aaron, I just want you to be happy. After I'm gone—"

"Stop. Just stop. I don't want to think about that."

"But we have to. As much as you don't want to, this isn't going to change. In a few more months, I won't be here."

Holt looked away for a moment and rubbed his eye. "We don't have to talk about this now."

"But that's what you always say. You've been avoiding this for months. And we don't have a lot of months left. And I just want to make sure you know. I know you're going to grieve for a while."

"Dee…"

"It's OK to be sad for a while. But I do want you to move on eventually. I want you to be happy. I want you to be open to finding love again. I don't want you to grow old, alone, cut off from the world. Finding someone else eventually doesn't mean forgetting about me. Or us. I want you to know that."

It was hard for Holt to think about any of that right now. Or maybe ever.

"I want you to promise me."

"Denise."

"No, I really want you to promise me. Not just give me lip-service. Please give me your word?"

Holt took a deep breath, not really wanting to agree to it, but also not wanting to make his wife unhappy, or make a promise that he didn't intend to keep.

"Aaron?"

Holt stared into her eyes and felt his heart melting. He didn't want to disappoint her. And she always had a way of breaking down his defenses.

"I promise."

"About?"

Holt sighed again. "That I'll... do my best to... not be alone for the rest of my life."

Denise smiled, gripping his hand a little tighter. "I know it's hard for you. Just do your best. For me?"

Holt faked a smile and nodded. "I will. I promise."

They gave each other a kiss, and pet Brutus, as they looked out at the water once more. It was a picturesque setting. The kind that belonged on a postcard. But sometimes, settings like these... it was just the calm before the storm. And a storm was rising. And it was barreling towards them like a Category 5 hurricane.

2

Holt was pushing his wife's wheelchair up the ramp to the porch when he noticed the black car pulling up. He let out a disapproving sigh as he immediately recognized the vehicle. It had been there before, though not lately. Holt figured it must have been about five or six months since they were last there.

Denise reached her hand up and put it on top of her husband's. "Just humor him for a few minutes, dear."

"Sure."

"I can take it from here."

Holt smiled and kissed her on the cheek. "I'll get Brutus."

As Denise wheeled herself into the house, Holt hopped off the porch, trying to pretend like the car wasn't even there. The driver's side door opened, and a man got out.

The man stood tall, his polished shoes clicking on the pavement as he approached Holt. He wore a tailored suit that exuded an air of authority, which he had, and his sharp gaze was fixed on Holt with unwavering intensity.

"Aaron," the man said in a voice that held a hint of elegance but also an underlying tone of danger. "Long time no see."

Holt's stomach churned as he recognized the man. It was Tom Barnes, one of The Nobody Man's CIA contacts. This unexpected visit could only mean one thing — trouble somewhere.

"What do you want?" Holt asked, trying to maintain a calm facade, though he already knew the answer. There was only one reason the man would be there.

"We need your help. The agency would like you to come in," Barnes replied. "We need The Nobody Man's expertise once again."

Holt walked right past him. "My answer's the same as it was the last time you were here."

Barnes walked after him. "It's been three years."

"I'm aware of that."

"When you said you needed some time…"

"It was for as long as I needed."

Holt reached the lake and bent down to scoop Brutus up in his arms. Barnes scrunched his eyebrows together, unsure what was happening.

"He always get the royal treatment?"

Holt briefly gave him the death stare. "He's dying. This is our routine every day."

Holt walked back to the house, with Barnes trying to keep up with him.

"Sorry to hear that. How much time's he got?"

"A few hours."

"Sorry, again. How's your wife doing?"

"Fine."

When they reached the house, Holt put Brutus down on the porch, gently stroking his head and face.

"Look, there are things going on."

"There are always things going on," Holt replied. "That won't change whether I'm back or not."

Barnes took a deep breath, his gaze shifting from Brutus to Holt.

"What's it going to take to bring you back?"

"There's nothing you can say."

Holt sighed, feeling the weight of the decision bearing down on him. He had spent the past three years trying to distance himself from the dangerous life he used to lead, focusing on taking care of Denise and enjoying what little time they had left together.

"I made a promise, Barnes," Holt said firmly. "I promised my wife, and myself, that I would give her the peace and quiet she deserves in her final days. I won't break that promise. Not for you. Not for the agency. Not for anyone."

Barnes nodded. "I understand."

"So there's really no reason to continue this conversation because my stance isn't changing."

Holt went inside, and with those parting words, and no one to talk to, Barnes turned and walked back to his car. He was a little huffy, but it was the reception and the answer he assumed he would get. As soon as the car had disappeared, Holt and Denise came back onto the patio, where they would spend the final few hours of Brutus' life together, as a family.

After leaving the vet's office, Holt found a curb to sit down on. He put his hand over his eyes and wiped the tears from them. Brutus had only been gone for a few minutes, but this weird feeling came over Holt's body. Like a piece of him was missing.

For the last fifteen years, Brutus had always been there. Even when Holt was gone on an assignment for a week or two, he could always count on that wagging tail greeting him once he came home. But now, he wouldn't be there.

Holt continued to sit there for a while, lost in his thoughts, and his heart heavy with grief. He looked at the spot next to him, almost expecting to see Brutus lying there, waiting to lick his hand as he often did. He felt guilty, even though he knew in his heart that he made the right decision. His eyes filled up with tears again, wondering if he should've waited another week or two.

But there was nothing he could do about that now. The decision was made, and he'd just have to push through it. And he still had Denise at home to worry about. Holt got back in his car and drove back to the house.

As he got near the property, with his window partially down, he could already smell the thick smoke. He also saw it rising in the air. He knew where it was coming from. The gray streak of smoke still stood out through the darkened sky.

Holt's heart pounded in his chest as he approached the property. The sight of the smoke sent a surge of adrenaline through his veins, replacing the grief for Brutus with a familiar sense of urgency. He pulled up to the house, his eyes widening at the intensity of the flames engulfing it.

Without hesitation, Holt jumped out of his car and sprinted towards the house, most of it already engulfed in flames.. As he neared, he could hear the crackling of the fire and feel its searing heat against his skin. Panic gripped him as he realized Denise might still be inside.

"Denise!" he yelled, taking a quick look around to see if she'd wheeled herself out somewhere.

Without getting a response, and not seeing her anywhere, the realization that she might still be inside hit him like a punch to the gut. Holt charged through the front door. Thick smoke filled the air, making it difficult to see and breathe, but he pressed on. He called out Denise's name, praying for a response.

"Denise!"

Once inside, he didn't have to go far to find his wife. Denise was lying there on the floor, completely out of her wheelchair, which was on its side. She was lying face down. But Holt noticed the blood around her. He turned her over, observing a bullet hole in the middle of her chest.

Holt's heart sank as he stared down at his wife's lifeless body. He kissed her on the lips as the flames danced around them, mocking him with their merciless destruction. Rage surged through his veins, fueled by grief and a burning desire for justice. He clenched his fists, his knuckles turning white as he fought to contain the torrent of emotions threatening to consume him. Tears streamed down his face as he continued to hold his wife's body in his arms.

With a heavy heart, he carefully lifted Denise's lifeless body and cradled her in his arms, shielding her from the heat and smoke as he made his way back towards the front door. As he stepped outside, Holt was greeted by a group of firefighters who had arrived to combat the fierce blaze. Their eyes widened with shock and sympathy as they saw the devastation that had befallen the once peaceful residence.

Holt laid Denise down gently on the grass, his gaze fixed on her. He whispered words of love to her, still not believing that she was gone. He looked back at the house as his mind raced, searching for answers amongst the heavy smoke and flickering flames. But right now, he didn't have any.

What he did have was a thirst for justice. For revenge. Someone extinguished the last few months remaining of his wife's life. It wasn't necessary. It didn't have to be. But someone did. And he wasn't going to let someone get away with that. No matter what it took, however long he had to search, he was going to find the person responsible. And he'd make them pay. He'd make sure, whoever it was, that they wished they never heard of The Nobody Man.

3

Langley, Virginia—Johnston was asked to go to Director Barnes' conference room. As she walked, she briefly put one of her hands on her stomach to try to quell her nerves. She walked past numerous colleagues, and quickly took her hand away, not wanting to give off the impression that she was nervous. But she was.

She didn't know what this meeting was about. She wasn't told, which was a little unusual. She'd been to a few of these meetings. But this time, she was going by herself. The other times, she'd been part of a team of individuals in there.

Josephine Johnston had been in the division for about a year, and while she enjoyed the job, every day she still felt like the rookie. She was treated like it, too. While she felt her contributions to the team were appreciated, and she was listened to, she was often reminded that she was on the low end of the totem pole.

But that never dampened her spirits. She was young, very bright, and had an upbeat personality. She wasn't yet beaten down by the numerous years on the job like most people had. She was determined to prove herself and make a name for herself within the division. And today was going to be her chance. She just didn't know it yet.

Once Johnston entered the briefing room, her eyes scanned the faces of her colleagues. There were eight other men and women around the table. The nerves quickly came back. The room was filled with experienced agents, each one exuding an aura of confidence and authority. She took a gulp, determined not to show her anxiety, and took her place among them, at the end of the table.

The room was silent as the door swung shut, most everyone looking down at the folders and papers they had on the table in front of them. Director Barnes stepped forward. As a seasoned veteran, his presence commanded respect from everyone in the room.

"Good morning, everyone," he began, his voice steady and authoritative. "I have called this meeting today to discuss a case that requires our utmost attention."

He had a clicker in his hand, which corresponded to a TV on the wall behind him. The picture of a man appeared, their first target of the day. Everyone started

The Nobody Man

writing down notes. Johnston was a little mesmerized, still not exactly sure what she was doing there. She took a look around the table and saw everyone writing. So she did the same, though hers would obviously be more of a jumbled mess than everyone else's.

An hour went by, and Johnston seemed as lost as ever. She was beginning to feel like she was invited there by mistake. They must have mixed the names up or something. This was a meeting for the higher-ups. The people that made decisions. She was not at that level.

It was too late to just walk out, though. She couldn't speak up and ask why she was there. That would be too embarrassing. Now her strategy, since she was close to the door, was that when the meeting ended, with everyone standing up, she'd quickly scoot out the door, with no one able to ask any questions about why she was there in the first place.

Mercifully, the meeting finally ended. Several agents spoke up, asking questions about their assignments. Thankfully, no questions were directed at Johnston, to which she would have had no idea what to say. Everyone began to stand up. Johnston quickly did the same, and was ready to bolt.

Barnes put his hand up. "Jo, if you could stay for a minute after everyone's gone?"

Johnston smiled and nodded. "Certainly."

She flashed an equally wide smile to the other agents as they all walked past her on the way out. She put her hand on her chin, looking down mostly, as she didn't want to look any further out of place than she already had.

"Selia, close the door on your way out, please," Barnes told the last person to leave.

Barnes and Johnston were the only people left in the room. He took a seat across from her. He slid a file folder across the table. She put her hand on top of it. Before she was able to open it, Barnes had a few more words for her.

"Before you open that, what is enclosed is highly classified. Only a handful of people are authorized to see what's inside."

Johnston took another gulp. Though she had security clearance, it sounded as if what was inside that folder went well above her pay grade.

Barnes smirked at her. "You're probably wondering what you're doing here."

"Uh, no. No, I was... well, maybe a little."

Barnes clasped his hands together on the table. "You've been with us, what... about a year?"

"Yes, sir, about that."

"You've been doing great work."

Johnston smiled, happy that she'd been recognized. Those were words that weren't heard that often around there.

"Thank you."

"It's been noticed," Barnes said. "By a lot of people,

including me. We think you're destined for bigger things."

Johnston looked rather uncomfortable hearing the accolades showered upon her. If she didn't know any better, she'd think she was getting the pink slip. This was about when the other shoe dropped.

"What would you say to... broadening your horizons? Getting a bigger piece of the puzzle?"

"Um, I guess I would say it depends on what was asked of me. Not that I wouldn't be grateful, but, I guess... I would just want to make sure I'm capable."

"You are. What would you say to rendezvousing with several field agents?"

Johnston raised her eyebrows, not sure if she was hearing correctly. "You want me to be a handler?"

Barnes winced, uncomfortable with the term. "Well, that's kind of an old-fashioned term. We would call it more of a Liaison Officer. You would interact with several field agents, make sure they have what they need to do their job. That sort of thing. What do you say?"

"I'm flattered to be considered. I'm just not sure I'm qualified to do the job. Most of my work has been behind a desk."

"Well, it will still be mostly behind a desk. Other than a few occasions here and there where you'll need to meet them in person... to check up on them, or pass them critical information that can only be done face-to-face. Most of your work will still be done behind the desk. Getting them whatever information they need, calling contacts, setting up itineraries, plans, escape plans, things of that nature. From what I can tell from the reports you've written, you're qualified."

Johnston took a few seconds to think, but knew this was her opportunity. She couldn't let it slip.

"Yeah. Yes. I'm in. I'm ready."

Barnes smiled. "Excellent. That file in front of you is your first challenge."

"Challenge?"

"Open it."

Johnston hesitated slightly, but did open it. Her eyes quickly went to the name of the person it belonged to, and swiftly brought her head back up.

"This is for real?"

Barnes nodded. "Aaron Holt. The Nobody Man."

Johnston's eyes went back to the file, engrossed in the contents. "I... I've heard rumors, like most people. I thought he was just a myth."

"No, he's very much real. He's been gone for three years. We want you to make contact with him to bring him back into the fold."

"Me?"

"Mmm hmm."

She could feel herself starting to sweat at the thought of talking to Holt. The man was almost a legend. She was... well, nobody. Why would he talk to her?

"At the risk of making myself sound... well, stupid,

I guess. Aren't there more experienced people to talk to him?"

"Believe me, we've tried. I talked to him myself just the other day. Other than me, we've had six or seven other people talk to him in these last three years. He's barely given any of us the time of day."

"Why do you think I would be any different?"

Barnes shrugged. "Different angle. Maybe you can appeal to him on a different level somehow."

Johnston was a little alarmed as she looked at the subsequent pages of Holt's file.

"It says here his wife was just... murdered?"

"Yeah. A couple of days ago."

It felt a little cold and callous to Johnston. Talking to a man about rejoining the agency so soon after having lost his wife.

"Are you sure now's the time to talk to him? I mean, maybe we should give him some space."

"Now's the perfect time," Barnes replied. "His wife was murdered. He's gonna want answers. Maybe we can help give him some as an incentive."

"We're going to use his wife... to help bring him back?"

"It seems cold, doesn't it? But unfortunately, we're not in the business of being warm and cozy. There are a lot of bad things happening out there. Things that Aaron Holt can stop. We need him back. And we need you to make it happen. Think you can do that?"

Johnston gulped, not sure whether she could or not. But somehow, she was going to have to.

"Yes, sir. I can do it."

Barnes stood up. "Good. We're counting on you."

Barnes opened the door and left the room. Johnston turned her head, making sure she was all alone. She let out a deep sigh. She put her hand on her forehead before looking down at the file again. She continued reading. And the more she read, the more she became convinced that she had no idea what she was getting herself into. She kept reading about Holt, and some of the assignments he'd been on. She was psyching herself out.

"Counting on me." She scratched the back of her head. "For some reason."

4

Holt stood at the foot of his wife's grave. The sun cast a warm glow over the cemetery, casting shadows that danced along the rows of the headstones. Holt stood there alone, his heart heavy with sorrow and anger. Denise's funeral had been a small affair, with no one else attending other than Holt. Neither Holt nor Denise had any family nearby.

As he stood there, lost in his thoughts, Holt looked up and saw a figure in the distance. She looked young, in her mid to late twenties, blonde hair, dressed in a business suit. She was leaning up against a tree, with her arms folded across her chest. She had her sights locked on Holt.

Holt already knew who she was. She had CIA written all over her. He didn't pay much more attention to her, though. Instead, Holt turned his attention back to the fresh grave before him. He knelt down, tracing his fingers over the engraved letters of Denise's name.

"I'm so sorry, Dee," he whispered, his voice barely audible above the rustling leaves. "You deserved better."

As tears welled up in his eyes, Holt was determined to find out who was responsible for this tragedy and make them pay. And he had a few ideas as to how he was going to do that. Now that his wife was laid to rest, Holt had a new sense of purpose. He rose to his feet and turned to face the blonde woman who had been watching him from afar. They locked eyes for a moment. Holt really had no interest in dealing with her at the moment.

Holt picked up a few blades of grass, and then tossed them onto the grave. He gave the blonde woman another glance, then turned and walked in the opposite direction. The woman hurried, hoping to catch up with him before he left.

Holt continued walking, his mind consumed by thoughts of revenge. He didn't want any other distractions, including talking to any junior agents. He assumed she'd been sent by Barnes to try to recruit him back into the world that he once left behind.

The woman quickened her pace, gaining ground on Holt. He could've hurried and left her behind, reaching his car before she was able to get to him, but he just didn't care enough to do that. Ignoring her was just as good an option. Despite his best efforts to ignore her, though, she persisted, determined to be seen and heard.

"Holt! Wait!"

Holt didn't respond. He didn't even turn his head to acknowledge her existence.

"Holt! Please, just give me a minute."

Holt rolled his eyes, knowing he shouldn't give her the time of day. But there was something in her voice. Something about it that he just had to acknowledge. It was a mix of friendliness and innocence. It was a weird combination for the CIA. He didn't come across it often in his time there.

"Who are you?"

"My name's Josephine Johnston."

"Barnes send you?"

"I'd really like to talk to you."

"I already told Barnes I wasn't coming back."

"Can I just have a few minutes of your time?"

"You've already got it. I'm sorry. There's nothing you can say to change my mind."

They reached his car. Holt turned his body to finally face her.

"In case you didn't get the memo, my wife was murdered."

There was sadness in her eyes. Holt felt he was a pretty good judge of character. In his line of work, you had to be. If you weren't, you'd wind up dead pretty quick. Either she was a pretty good actor, or her personality was completely different from Barnes'. Not that it mattered.

"I know that," Johnston said. "I'm sorry. I really am. Is there anything we can do for you?"

"The only thing you can do for me is stay out of my way."

Holt opened the car door and got in behind the wheel. He rolled down his window.

"What do you plan on doing?"

There was no delay in Holt's response. "Whatever I have to."

Holt drove away, knowing that Johnston wouldn't have enough time to get back to her car and follow him. Of course, there could have been another car out there waiting to tail him, but he knew how to spot a tail. He drove around aimlessly for a while, making sure there was nobody following him. There wasn't. He was in the clear.

He didn't want anyone knowing where he was going or what he was doing. Holt drove to a small internet cafe. He had a specific purpose in mind. Once inside, he found an open computer and logged on. He typed in the internet address of where his cloud security camera footage was stored. He logged in and filtered the results to the night Denise was murdered. He could've done this on his phone, but he preferred the larger screen and a desk where he could take notes if he needed to.

As Holt sifted through the footage, his heart

pounded in his chest. The images flickered on the screen, each frame a potential clue that could lead him closer to the truth. He watched as the minutes ticked by, his eyes scanning for any suspicious activity.

And then, he saw it. The outline of a man lurking in the shadows just outside the range of the camera. The person moved with stealth and purpose, their features obscured by darkness. Holt's pulse quickened as he rewound the footage, trying to catch a glimpse of the person's face.

But no matter how many times he replayed the video, the figure remained just out of focus. Frustration gnawed at Holt's insides, a deep-seated anger bubbling to the surface. He couldn't let this mysterious individual slip through his fingers. He had him. He was there. He had to get a cleaner shot of him.

Holt had numerous cameras set up on the property, all secretly placed, hidden to the untrained or unsuspecting eye. Dozens of cameras. With his past, there was no way he wouldn't. He kept switching cameras to try to get a better glimpse of the man. There wasn't one. At least in the moments before the fire.

Holt then adjusted the time to the moments after the fire started. If he didn't get a shot of the man going in, maybe he would going out. He checked out each camera in detail. He took no picture for granted, even if there appeared to be nothing there.

Then, he saw the man again. This time, it was a

much better shot. It was a different camera this time. Holt froze the video and zoomed in to get a better look at him. The man never turned his face fully to look at the camera, but it was a pretty good side view of him. And he was wearing a hat. A red baseball hat. Probably more like burgundy. There was something written on the front. A logo of some sort. But Holt couldn't quite make it out. He quickly jotted down any distinguishing details he could gather from the footage: height, build, mannerisms. Every little piece could form a puzzle and lead to a bigger picture.

Holt continued to scrutinize the footage, determined to extract any possible clues. There had to be something that could lead him to this mysterious man with the red hat. He played the video over and over again, his eyes glued to the screen, searching for any minute detail that he might have missed. There didn't seem to be anything else, though.

He went through every possible camera angle for the next few hours, hoping to find something else. Someone else. But he didn't. All he could find was the one man. But that was enough for now. At least he had that. He had a starting point.

Holt printed out the photos he had of the mysterious man on his property. With the details he had gathered, Holt knew he needed to find out more about this individual. Was he working alone? Or was he hired by someone? Either way, it was obviously someone from Holt's past. This wasn't a random act of violence. Someone targeted him. Or, more accurately, targeted the person he cared about and loved the most.

Holt closed the browser and left the internet cafe. Once back in his car, he looked down at the passenger seat, where he had the notes and pictures he just took. If he talked to enough people, looked under enough rocks, someone would know this guy. Someone would give him up. It was just a matter of sticking with it. And Holt wasn't going to let this go. He wasn't going to let it slide. He'd find this guy. No matter how long it took.

5

Before going or doing anything else, Holt took a trip back home. With what he was about to embark on, it was probably the last he'd see of it for a while. He wanted to soak it all in before he went on this manhunt. If there was one thing he knew about whoever this guy with the red hat was, he probably wasn't hanging around very long.

When Holt pulled up in his driveway, he saw another car already sitting there. He had a view of the inside, and no one was in it. Holt had a clear view of the backyard, as they had no fence, and could see the outline of a person sitting down by the lake.

Holt took a deep breath, just sitting there for a moment. He then got out, and slowly walked down to the lake. Johnston had her back to him, sitting on a large rock. His mood crossed between annoyance that the woman couldn't seem to take a hint, and admiration that she didn't seem to give up. He could at least respect it, even if it bothered him to see her again.

Johnston knew Holt was nearby without even having to turn around to look at him. She could hear the crunching of the leaves under his feet, a few twigs breaking under his shoes. She continued looking out at the water. Holt put his hands in his pockets and stood next to her, though there was a few feet of distance between them. His eyes focused on the lake, as well.

"I can see why you've lived here. So very peaceful."

Holt cleared his throat, helping to prevent some tears from flowing as he thought of his wife.

"Used to be."

Johnston turned her head slightly, glancing at Holt. She could see the pain etched on his face, the sorrow in his eyes. She wanted to reach out, to offer some comfort, but she knew better than to intrude on his grief. Instead, she kept her gaze fixed on the serene waters of the lake.

"I am very for your loss," Johnston said, speaking softly, her voice barely audible above the gentle rustle of the leaves. "I know it doesn't mean much, but if there's anything I can do to help..."

Holt's eyes flickered towards Johnston, his expression guarded. His instinct was still to push her away. He knew why she was there. They'd sent her to bring him in.

"Why don't you just come out with it and tell me

what you really want?" Holt asked, his voice laced with skepticism.

Johnston looked at him, almost a little angry at his tone. It felt a little heartless hearing that she might have ulterior motives. But after a brief thought, couldn't blame him under the current conditions. She wasn't just there to offer moral support. She took a gulp.

"Do you know how many other agents they've sent over the years to have this conversation?"

Johnston looked down for a moment. "No, not exactly."

Holt looked at the lake, as far as he could see. "I think you're the eighth. You're the first new person, though. Guess they're changing tactics. Grasping at straws."

"What's that supposed to mean?"

Holt looked at her again. "How long have you been on the job?"

"I'm not fresh out of spy school, if that's what you mean."

"You're not experienced, either."

"And what makes you think that?"

"I can just tell. You don't have that obnoxious aura around you yet, like you know everything. And you're not hardened yet by all the atrocities this world has to offer."

Johnston was silent for a few seconds. She looked at him out of the corner of her eye.

"I'm not sure I've ever been insulted so nicely before."

The faintest of a smile crept over Holt's face.

"I didn't mean it as an insult," Holt said, his voice softer than before. "It's just... there's a certain weariness that comes with experience. A heaviness that settles deep in your soul after you've seen and experienced too much. And you haven't been burdened by it yet."

"I know it may seem like I'm just another agent that's been sent to fetch you and bring you back in. But I genuinely want to help. I know you've got a lot going on right now. A lot of emotions. I'm not asking you to make a decision right now. I'm just asking that maybe you think about it?"

"Why do they want me back so bad? You know that?"

"I think you probably already know the answer to that, don't you?"

Holt laughed to himself, picking up a few blades of grass. "Yeah. I guess I do."

"You have gifts. Talents other people don't have."

"Gifts, huh? Three years of solitude, of watching the person you love most in this world slowly fade away, maybe that softens a man. Did you ever think that maybe I'm not the same man I used to be?"

"The agency thinks you are."

"They would say and do anything that benefits

them an inch. I wouldn't trust them as far as I can spit."

"So what are your plans now?" Johnston asked.

"I dunno. Thought I might go fishing."

"Fishing?"

Holt looked up at the sky. "Fishing helps clear a person's mind sometimes."

He turned to leave. Johnston jumped up off the rock.

"Where are you going?"

"Told you," Holt said. "Gotta go buy a line. Mine got a little crispy."

Holt briskly walked back to his car, followed by Johnston once again. She was determined to not let him drive off on her again.

"Can we at least talk again?"

Holt got inside his car and put his window down. "I'll tell you what. Meet me here again tomorrow."

Holt drove off, heading to his storage unit. The storage unit was a place Holt hadn't visited in three years. The moment he stepped away, he put everything from his former life in there. Boxes, notes, weapons, memories. They were all there.

As he unlocked the padlock, he felt a certain weight on his shoulders. The weight of his past. He lifted the door open and stepped inside, a wave of nostalgia hitting him. The room, a medium-sized unit, was only about half-filled.

Holt made his way to some of the boxes and opened them. He took out several stacks of notebooks and case files, each containing bits and pieces of information that had consumed his life over the years. It was here, amidst the faded ink and yellowed pages, that he hoped to find answers to the questions that haunted him.

He pulled out an old journal and began flipping through its worn pages, searching for any clues related to the red-hatted man he had seen on the surveillance footage. The entries described countless encounters with shady individuals, and potential suspects who could be linked to Denise's murder. The link was here somewhere. Holt knew it.

As he tossed a few boxes around, he came across one that held several weapons inside. There were several pistols, along with some ammunition. He'd just picked up one of the Glocks, jammed a magazine into it, and put it in the back of his pants, when he heard the sound of a woman clearing her throat.

Holt turned around to find Johnston standing at the entrance of the storage unit, a mixture of concern and apprehension etched across her face. She glanced at the loaded Glock in Holt's waistband and raised an eyebrow.

"What exactly do you think you're doing?" Johnston asked, her voice laced with a hint of worry. "Looks like you're loaded for bear."

Holt shrugged nonchalantly, trying to maintain a facade of indifference. "What I'm doing is not your business."

Johnston took a step forward, her eyes fixed on the gun. "Look, I get that you're hurting and desperate for answers. But arming yourself like this... it's not going to bring Denise back. It won't bring you peace."

Holt's grip on the Glock tightened as he stared at Johnston. His expression hardened. "How would you know what will bring me peace?"

"You're right, I don't. I'm sorry."

"I don't need your lectures. This is my way of finding justice for Denise. I won't rest until I catch the person that killed her."

Johnston smiled, trying to ease the tension. "So much for fishing, huh?"

Holt glanced up at her, then went back to his boxes. "What are you doing here, anyway? You followed me?"

"Maybe. You forgot to give me a time for our meeting tomorrow."

Holt briefly stopped, his eyes moving towards her for a moment. She was quick.

"I almost believed it. But then I thought, would a man like you really go fishing at a time like this?"

"I'm fishing for something. But it's not in any water."

"Maybe I could help."

Holt stopped his movements again, putting his hands on the sides of the boxes in a defensive posture.

"Look, I don't need anyone's help. And I don't need you offering to do something for me in the hopes of getting in good with me so I'll break down and join you and your crusade later. I'm done with that."

"I wasn't. And I was under the impression that there weren't any leads. I also somehow get the feeling that you know something nobody else does."

Holt brushed her off and continued looking through some of the notebooks.

Johnston walked further into the room. "What exactly are you looking for?"

"I don't know yet."

She stopped at one of the boxes and looked inside. "I'm really good at analyzing things."

"That what you did before they latched you onto me? Analyst?"

She grabbed one of the notebooks, but was careful to not open it without his permission. "I'm just saying. If you tell me what you're looking for, maybe I can help?"

He briefly stopped and looked at the notebook in her hand. His voice softened.

"I don't know."

"Then how will you know if you find it?"

Holt could only shake his head, not really having an answer for her. She held the notebook up further.

"May I?"

He gulped as he looked at it, then at her. He gave sort of a sheepish nod. She had more questions as she looked through the notebook, fascinated by some of his notes.

"What is it that you're not saying? What do you know?"

Holt sighed and lowered the book he was looking at. "Look, I don't trust you."

"You don't know me."

"That's right, I don't. But I don't trust the people you work for. And your interests aren't the same as mine. Right now, I'm only interested in finding out who killed my wife. Your only interest in my situation is whether you can use it to help bring me back in. That puts us with different agendas. Now, I'm sorry to be blunt, and I don't mean to be insulting, but we do not have the same goals here."

Johnston licked her lips, as she felt her mouth getting dry. As hard as it was to hear that, she couldn't deny the truth in it. They did have different motives. Even if she was sympathetic to his situation, and even if she truly did want to help, he was correct in his assessment.

She continued looking through one of the books. "I see a lot of names here. Do you think one of them is responsible?"

"I don't know. I haven't ruled out the possibility that you people are behind it."

The Nobody Man

Johnston looked horrified at the suggestion. "You really think we might have murdered your wife?"

"You guys have been trying to get me back for years. She dies, and magically you show up again. Coincidence?"

Johnston shook her head. "No. I wouldn't be party to something like that."

"Knowingly, maybe."

"Why would we take the risk? Without wanting to sound cold and thoughtless, and I hate myself for even talking like this, but your wife only had a few more months to live. Why take the chance of pissing you off and making an enemy of you just to get you back a few months early? The agency has waited this long. They could wait a little longer."

He couldn't argue with that logic. He gave a slight nod and went back to the notebook. After only a few more seconds, he tore a page out of the book and put it in his pocket. He put the other notebooks in the box, including the one in Johnston's hand, and put the lid on it. He then walked towards the entrance.

Johnston looked confused. He obviously had found something. Something he wasn't interested in sharing. She jogged after him.

"So what'd you find?"

Once they got to the door, Holt turned around to face her. "Look, so far, you seem like a nice person. I got no issue with you yet. But if you follow me again, you and I are gonna have problems, you understand?"

Johnston nodded. "I do. I won't follow you."

"And I also expect to find this storage locker the same way as I left it. If I find the lock cut off or boxes sorted through, we're gonna have an ever bigger problem. Do I make myself clear?"

Johnston put her hands behind her back, as if she were in the army taking orders. "Totally."

"All right, then."

They stepped outside the unit, and Holt closed the door, putting his padlock back on it.

"Could you use a hand?"

Holt's shoulders slumped, feeling like she wasn't getting the message. She read his body language and wanted to ease his fears. She put her hands out.

"Just wait." She reached into her pocket and removed her business card. She stuck it out, hoping Holt would take it. "If you need anything... anything... just call me. Maybe I can help."

Holt glanced down at the card with trepidation. He didn't want to take anything from anybody. And he definitely didn't want anyone's help. She could see he was hesitant.

"Look, no favors owed, and no expectations about you coming back. If you need me for just one thing, and then we never talk to each other again, that's fine. I'll be disappointed, but I'll get over it."

Holt continued looking at the card, still not making a move for it.

"You never know when you might need a friend. And like I said, no expectations."

Holt sighed, and then reluctantly took the card. He held the card up for a moment, then put it in his back pocket. He turned and walked away.

"I'll see ya."

"I hope so," Johnston replied. She stood still, watching him until he was no longer in sight. "I certainly hope so."

6

Munich, Germany – Detlef Altmann was sitting in his favorite restaurant, having a conversation with one of his business associates. He had several guards seated at nearby tables, as was the usual. Altmann was a major player in the German underworld. And someone that Holt had dealings with before.

Though he himself was never on The Nobody Man's radar, Altmann's son was. Altmann contained his dealings to his own operation, which was big in German circles, but was not really a blip on the radar in terms of what the CIA was looking for in the world view.

His son, though, had bigger aspirations. He always did. Friedrich Altmann was a dreamer. He always dreamed of taking what his father started and going bigger. Instead of only being the big fish in a German

The Nobody Man

pond, Friedrich wanted to be known world-wide. Unfortunately, he accomplished that goal a little too well.

He got mixed up with terror organizations, major drug suppliers, the sex trade, and big-time gun traffickers. He made the big-time. But that always comes at a cost. While he became a bigger name, he also fell onto the CIA's radar. And whenever that happens, eventually, there will be a bullet with your name on it. And that bullet came courtesy of The Nobody Man.

Of course, whenever events like that go down, there are always rumors. People speculating on who, or why. Eventually, word got back to Detlef Altmann that The Nobody Man was responsible. It was Holt's last mission before he left the agency.

The loss of a child could make people do crazy things. Maybe even more than the loss of a spouse. And men like Altmann had long memories. He'd never forget something like that. He swore he'd find out who The Nobody Man was and make him pay. He swore he'd get even someday. Maybe now, he finally had.

Altmann had enough power, money, and connections to worm his way into Holt's inner circle. All he had to do was get the right kind of dirt, or enough money, to bribe a lower-level person to find the information he needed. He wasn't above doing that.

Holt had been watching Altmann and his associate for the last thirty minutes, just waiting for the right time to approach. And, like usual, he had blended into his surroundings. As Altmann took the last remaining sip of water from his drink, Holt moved in. Nobody suspected a thing. Holt looked like all the other waiters in the restaurant.

With a pitcher of water in his hand, Holt casually walked over to the table, and lifted the glass off the table. Neither Altmann nor his guest paid the man any attention. Holt filled the glass with water and put it back down on the table. He walked away, heading towards the back of the restaurant, where he put the pitcher down, then walked out through the back. His work there was done.

A minute later, Altmann reached for his glass and picked it up. He took a sip, but as he was about to put it back down, saw a small, folded up piece of paper lying where his glass had been. His arm froze mid-air, the glass hanging there, as he stared at the paper.

Finally, he put the glass down, and picked the paper up. He unfolded it to see what it was. There was only a phone number. Altmann slowly turned his head, his eyes scanning the restaurant to see who could have given him this. It had to have been the waiter that was just there. He didn't see him now.

Altmann's eyes went back to the note. He stared at that number. Who was leaving him this? And why? He wasn't sure he wanted to call it, but he knew he had to. After a couple of minutes, he concluded his business, and sent his associate on his way. He then took out his phone and called the number.

Holt was sitting on a bench further down the street, the front door of the restaurant still within his view. He had his phone in his hand. It was a new one he picked up at the airport after he flew in. As soon as the phone rang, Holt answered.

"Who is this?" Altmann asked in German.

"I know you speak English, Detlef."

The concern was plainly evident in Altmann's voice. "Who are you?"

"I'm sure if you think long and hard enough, you'll know the answer to that."

"You could be anyone."

"I hear you've been looking for me for a long time," Holt said.

"I've been looking for a lot of people."

"I doubt they're the ones that killed your son."

Altmann fell silent on the other end of the line, the weight of Holt's words sinking in.

"You're him."

"Yes, I'm him. And we need to talk."

"What for? One member of the family isn't good enough for you?"

"I need to talk to you."

"That's what we're doing, isn't it?"

"Not here," Holt said. "Not on the phone. Needs to be in person."

"Why?"

"You won't be as likely to lie to me in person."

"And what makes you think I'll agree to this?"

"Because you know who I am. If I wanted you dead yet, I'd have killed you where you're sitting."

"And if I refuse to meet?"

"Then we'll be meeting again soon, anyway. And I guarantee our encounter will be more than me slipping you a piece of paper."

Altmann really didn't feel safe meeting him. But he also knew who he was talking to. He wiped the sweat off his face. The man on the phone was right. If The Nobody Man wanted him dead, he would be. He might as well take his chances.

"Fine. Come back in and we'll talk."

"You and me alone," Holt said. "Without your guards. Down by the river. Across from the concert hall."

"When?"

"One hour. If I see someone that works for you, I'll kill you on the spot."

Holt hung up, not wanting to give Altmann the chance to respond, or negotiate. By the sound of his voice, Holt could tell that Altmann was nervous. Unfortunately, he also wasn't sure Altmann was the guy he was looking for. He sounded too scared to be. Of course, maybe he was just scared that he'd been discovered to actually be the one that ordered it.

That was why Holt wanted to meet him in person. He wanted to talk to him face to face. He wanted to

The Nobody Man

look Altmann in the eye. Then he'd know. Then he'd be sure.

It would only take about twenty minutes to get to the meeting spot. Holt left his position and would get there first. He wanted to observe the area for a bit until Altmann got there. Once he was, Holt would be able to tell if any of his cronies were there with him, milling around.

When Holt arrived, he waited under the bridge. Altmann got there ahead of schedule, arriving twenty minutes early. The crime boss went straight for a railing overlooking the Rhine River. Holt left him to his own devices for a little while. His eyes were scanning the area for signs of Altmann's men hovering nearby. It looked clear. He didn't notice anyone. Certainly not the guys that were with Altmann at the restaurant.

Holt moved toward Altmann, almost surprising the man when he got near him. Altmann was wide-eyed as he looked the secret assassin over.

"You're The Nobody Man?"

Holt kept his head moving, always on the lookout. "I don't like to advertise."

"I figured you'd be taller."

Holt almost let out a smile, slightly amused by the comment.

"You know, for a while, I dreamed of this moment."

Holt didn't reply. He just stared at him.

"I dreamed of the day where you'd be within arm's reach of me. Then I would kill you for what you did."

Holt didn't look worried. "Looks like you got your wish."

Altmann made a face and looked at the river. "It was a fleeting moment. The pain of a grieving father talking." He took a moment to collect himself. "So what brings you here?"

"More of a question, really. A few days ago, someone very close to me was killed. I wanna know if you're the one behind it."

Altmann raised an eyebrow as he looked at him. He could hardly believe it.

"I don't even know your name. How would I kill someone you know?"

"Rumors a few years ago were that you were looking for me."

Altmann moved his head and arms around, basically confirming it.

"I won't deny it. I was. But that was three years ago. Six months later, I stopped."

"Why?" Holt asked.

"Because I hit nothing but dead ends. I couldn't find out from anyone who The Nobody Man was. No one was talking. Then, as time passed, some of the pain faded away. I stopped thinking with my heart."

"Meaning?"

"We are all in this business knowing there are inherited risks. You, me, my son, all of us. You get into this knowing what kind of fate may await you at some point. There are police, rivals, arrests, assassinations, betrayal, the list goes on and on. Once the pain faded, I thought rationally. My son's death... was just business. I realized it wasn't personal. He got involved in things he was not prepared for. I warned him against doing so. But he was determined to make his own path. To go bigger. It was foolish. That was what cost him his life. You were just the one that pulled the trigger. If it wasn't you, it would have been someone else."

As the man talked, Holt could see it in his eyes, and in his mannerisms. Altmann wasn't responsible for his wife's death. He spoke like an intelligent man. He didn't speak like someone who was consumed by revenge. And that was the man he needed to find. Altmann turned to look at Holt squarely in the eyes.

"Tell me. Who is this person you lost?"

Holt hesitated for a second, not sure if he should reveal it. In the end, though, he figured there was no point in hiding it. He looked down for a moment.

"My wife."

"It pains you greatly," Altmann said. "I know that look. I saw it every day in the mirror for six months. You are now looking for the person responsible."

"I am."

"Why do you think it is me?"

"That's why I'm here. To find out."

Altmann shook his head. "Some might think I'm crazy. But I no longer wish to kill you. But even if I did,

I would not come after your wife. I would come after you."

"I kill your son. You kill my wife for revenge?"

"Was your wife involved in this life?"

"No."

"Then it is senseless. Friedrich was not innocent. I am not innocent. You are not innocent. But your wife? That is going to a level in which I would not go."

Holt stared at the man, his words really hitting him. He didn't believe Altmann was lying to him. He seemed like a man who was speaking genuinely and honestly. He wasn't hiding anything.

"It was to my knowledge no one knew your real name?"

"Very few people do," Holt answered.

"I would start your search there. One of them must be responsible."

"Maybe so."

"Or maybe it was your employer. Ever think maybe they could do such a thing?"

"It's occurred to me."

"Perhaps you have a bigger problem, though."

"Yeah? How you figure?"

"Whatever you've done, you angered someone terribly. But it's worse than that. The person responsible for this, they're not just interested in revenge for some past transgression. They're interested in torturing you. If it was revenge, they would just come

The Nobody Man

after you. This... this is something more. They want to make you suffer."

They talked for a little while longer, with both of them eventually going their separate ways. Holt continued walking along the river, though. The water helped bring some peace and clarity to his troubled mind. He thought about everything that Altmann told him. He was right. This was about making him suffer.

Holt just assumed that whoever killed Denise was really after him. When they got to the house, saw he wasn't there, decided to kill Denise just for spite. But what if that was actually the plan? What if they purposefully waited for a time when Holt wouldn't be there so they could target his wife?

He couldn't get his mind around that, though. Why? Why would someone want to do that? What reason could there be? Altmann was right about one other thing. This wasn't just about The Nobody Man. This was about Aaron Holt. This was about someone who knew his real name. And that was a much shorter list. And it was about time he found out some answers.

7

Marsala, Sicily – Holt once again didn't waste time with hotels. He had his sights set on one man. Giorgio Pelligrini. He was an Italian who assisted Holt on numerous assignments. He was a CIA informant, who Holt used often while in the region. Holt considered him a trusted friend. Well, as trusted as someone could be in this line of work.

Pelligrini knew Holt's real name. The Nobody Man talked to Pelligrini more than he did most of the people in the CIA. But Holt hadn't talked to him in some time. Three years, to be precise. Once Holt gave up the life to be with Denise, he left everything in the rearview mirror.

He wouldn't have thought Pelligrini would be the one to sell him out. But, three years can change a lot of people. They weren't close anymore. And now, Pelligrini was at the top of the list. At the moment, he was Holt's chief suspect.

Holt arrived at Giorgio Pelligrini's modest villa, hidden among the vineyards of Marsala. It was a warm evening, and the scent of ripened grapes hung in the air. The sun was beginning to set, casting a soft orange glow over the sprawling estate.

As he approached the villa, Holt couldn't help but feel a sense of nostalgia. He'd been there before. Numerous times as he and Pelligrini went over plans for a mission, or decided on an attack strategy, or an exit path. He and Pelligrini shared many successful missions together, forming an unspoken bond of trust and camaraderie. In this business, you learned to trust very few people. Pelligrini was one of those who broke through the restraints. But now, that trust was replaced by suspicion and doubt.

Holt's grip tightened around the handle of his gun concealed beneath his jacket. He knew he had to proceed with caution. If Pelligrini had indeed betrayed him, there was no telling what awaited him beyond those elegant doors. The good thing was that since Holt had been there, he knew the best place to enter. Pelligrini had a security system in place, but Holt knew the blind spots.

On the northwest corner of the property, there was a tree where the branches hung low. Someone could use that to get over the fence, all out of view of the security camera. Holt mentioned cutting the tree down to Pelligrini before, but the man always persisted in leaving it the way it was. He loved that tree. Even if it was a security problem.

Stepping onto the cobblestone path leading to the entrance, Holt mentally prepared himself for any scenario that might unfold. Memories of past missions flooded his mind — moments of danger, adrenaline-pumping pursuits through which Pelligrini helped smuggle him out of a few jams. But Holt had to put all that out of his mind now. At the moment, Pelligrini was a suspect in his wife's murder. Until they could be cleared, everyone was.

Holt hurried to the northwest corner of the property and reached the tree. He carefully climbed over the fence, making sure not to make any noise. He landed gracefully on the other side and stealthily made his way towards the villa. His senses heightened, every nerve in his body on high alert.

As he approached the back entrance, a small window caught Holt's attention. It was slightly ajar, offering a glimpse into Pelligrini's study. His curiosity piqued, Holt crouched down and peered inside. The study was dimly lit, with shelves lined with old books and maps. A large wooden desk dominated the room, cluttered with papers and various gadgets. But there was no sign of Giorgio Pelligrini.

Holt hesitated for a moment, debating whether to continue with his original plan or investigate further and slip in through the window. He knew he couldn't afford any missteps, especially if Pelligrini truly was involved in Denise's murder. With his gun still firmly in hand, he crept towards the back entrance of the villa. He could always go back to the window if needed.

It was unlocked. The door creaked softly as Holt pushed it open, revealing a dimly lit corridor. He slipped inside, closing the door behind him as silently as possible. The air felt heavy with anticipation, and every noise seemed magnified in the silence. The house was covered in tile flooring. Pelligrini hated carpet.

Moving stealthily through the hallway, Holt's senses heightened. He couldn't hear a single sound coming from anywhere. The eeriness of the silence filled Holt with uneasiness. He knew that Pelligrini was a meticulous man, always prepared for any situation. The absence of any noise made him question if he had been too hasty in suspecting his old friend. But doubt lingered in the back of his mind, gnawing at him like a persistent ache.

Holt cautiously made his way towards the study, where he had caught a glimpse through the window. With each step, he braced himself for a confrontation, prepared to defend himself if necessary. As he neared the open doorway, his eyes darted around, searching for any signs of movement or danger.

Entering the study, the room was empty, save for the scattered papers and discarded gadgets on the desk. But something was off. The room wasn't neat and tidy. That wasn't the Giorgio Pelligrini that Holt knew. The man couldn't deal with a messy room. Not even a piece of paper on the floor that missed the trash can. A book turned on its side on the bookshelf instead of standing upright. A folder on the desk with some of its contents hanging out the side. Everything needed to be neat.

But as Holt looked around, there were papers all over the desk, as if someone had been looking for something. The bookshelf... all the books looked like they'd been sorted through. This wasn't the way Pelligrini would have left it. Not on his own.

Holt continued looking through the house. None of the other rooms quite looked like the study did. But there were little things that Holt noticed. A picture hanging a little crooked, dirty plates in the sink, clothes not put away in the closet. This wasn't the house of the man he knew.

After searching through the top two floors, Holt ventured down to the basement. It was mostly a wine cellar, where Pelligrini had a collection of several thousand bottles. As he descended the steps, Holt removed his gun, getting an eerie feeling he was about to find trouble. There was a distinct odor.

The basement was dimly lit, the only source of light coming from a small window on a far wall. Rows and rows of wine bottles were neatly organized on wooden shelves, from the floor to the ceiling, creating a maze that stretched out in the darkness. Holt's footsteps echoed softly as he cautiously moved deeper into the cellar. The air grew colder, sending a shiver down his spine.

His heart raced with apprehension, anticipating what he might find. The air down here hung heavy with a musty scent, mingled with the rich aroma of aged wine. Along with the other smell that Holt was all-too familiar with. It was an eerie atmosphere, intensifying the feeling of foreboding that enveloped Holt. He gripped his gun tighter, his senses on high alert.

As Holt rounded a corner, his eyes fell upon a sight that made his blood run cold. There, bound and gagged in the corner of the cellar, was Giorgio Pelligrini. His face was bruised and bloodied, his clothes torn, his body slumped forward as if he had been struggling against his restraints.

Holt slowly walked over to Pelligrini. He knew there was no hurry. He put his fingers on Pelligrini's neck to check for a pulse. There was none. He was dead. And judging from how cold Pelligrini's body was, and the smell, he'd been dead for at least a week.

Holt holstered his gun and started checking around, hoping to find some kind of clue as to who had done this. He went back upstairs to check the study again. That was where Pelligrini did most of his business. Maybe there was something there.

Holt meticulously combed through the study, carefully examining every inch of the room. He pulled out drawers, overturned books, and unfolded crumpled papers, searching for any clue that could lead him to the identity of Pelligrini's killer. As he combed through the room, he couldn't shake off the feeling that someone had been one step ahead of him. There just didn't seem to be anything there.

Just as Holt was beginning to lose hope, his eyes caught a glimmer of something underneath a stack of papers on the desk. Something he missed the first time through it. After carefully removing the sheets, he discovered a small, handwritten note tucked away beneath them. It was written in code. But it wasn't any code that Holt was familiar with. He and Pelligrini sometimes communicated in code, a prerequisite for the job. But this was different. This was a combination of numbers and letters, along with a few other symbols mixed in for good measure. It didn't make sense to him.

Holt went through the room one more time, just to make sure there wasn't anything else he overlooked. But there wasn't. All he could find was this one piece of paper with a code on it.

Holt stared at it. This might've had to do with Denise's death. Or maybe it was completely unrelated. Was Pelligrini tortured and killed to find out The Nobody Man's real name? Or did he just get himself involved in another situation that he couldn't find a way out of? Right now, it was still unclear.

The Nobody Man

But at least Holt had the code. Whether he could do anything with it was another matter. But he had something.

Holt found a motel room not too far away, where he took out his laptop and started going to work. He began trying to decipher the code, though he wasn't having much luck with it. He spent hours going over it. Nothing was sticking. Tired, he was close to calling it a night and picking it back up in the morning.

He reached into his bag and noticed Johnston's card sticking out. He debated the merits of calling her. He didn't want to be indebted to her. Or to anyone. Especially no one at the agency. He didn't want a cloud hanging over his head. But as he looked at the code, he thought he was going to need help with it. And right now, he wasn't sure there was anyone else he could trust.

Until this was sorted out, and he knew who was behind it, he couldn't go to any of his former contacts. Not until he knew it was safe. And while he didn't completely trust Johnston yet either, at least not on a professional level, he at least felt sure she had nothing to do with it.

Holt wrestled with the decision for a while. He looked at the phone, then the code, and kept flipping between the two for a good ten minutes. Finally, he decided to bite the bullet. He picked up his phone. His regular one. He was using a burner one if he needed to contact anyone on his journey, like he did with Altmann. After a few rings, Johnston picked up.

"Josephine Johnston."

"Does that offer to help still stand?"

"Aaron? Hi! Yes, of course it does. What do you need?"

"I'm sorry to call you so late. Hopefully I didn't disturb you or anything."

Johnston raised an eyebrow and looked out her window. "Well, it's getting a little dark, but I'm not usually in the habit of packing it in at six."

Holt rubbed his face. "Ah, I'm sorry. I forgot about the time difference."

"Where are you?"

"Not important. But I found something. I'm not sure if it has anything to do with my situation, or something else, but I can't seem to crack it."

"What is it?"

"Some type of code. I can't break it. It's not familiar to me."

"Sure, send it over. I'll start working on it."

Holt hesitated in his response. "Uh, can we just keep this between us for now?"

"You still don't trust us?"

Holt wanted to choose his words carefully. "Look, I don't know what's going on. Or what this is about. Right now, I can't afford to trust too many people. The only thing I'm fairly certain of is that you're not involved. If you ever have hopes of me rejoining the agency, I'm gonna need to trust you. That starts now."

Johnston cleared her throat. "OK, well, I might still need to bring a few other people on board to help decipher this code. But, um, I don't have to tell anyone it's from you. I can just say it's from a… an anonymous source for now. At least until we know more."

"I guess that's good enough."

"When can you get me this code? I'll start working on it right away."

"I'll take a picture and send it to you," Holt replied.

"If I get anything, where can I reach you?"

"This number."

"Are you in any kind of trouble right now?"

"Nah. I'm fine."

"Is there anything else I can do for you?"

"Nope. Just figuring out that code will be good enough."

"Where'd you get it?"

"Found it."

"That's all you're gonna give me?" Johnston asked.

"For now."

"OK. I'll get right on it. Hopefully, I'll have something for you tomorrow."

"Thank you."

Holt hung up and put his phone down. He reached into his pocket and removed a picture of Denise. He sat down in a well-worn chair in the corner. He stared at his wife's picture.

"I miss you."

His eyes were getting glossy as he thought about all the moments they shared. Moments they would never have again. And while he'd been trying to prepare himself for these days for months, it was different now. The way it ended was so sudden. He wasn't prepared for that.

"I thought I was done with the man I used to be." His eyes sunk to the floor. "But I'm not. I can't be."

Holt closed his eyes, putting the picture of his wife on his chest. He quickly drifted off to sleep, dreaming of the moment he'd find the person responsible for ending her life too soon. And putting a bullet through their head.

8

Johnston glanced over each of her shoulders, making sure no one was watching. Not that anyone should have been. She put the piece of paper with the code that Holt found next to her keyboard. She put it through several programs the CIA used to help decipher codes. It didn't match any known code that they had on file. She kept at it, though.

After several hours, she decided to enlist some help. She got together with a few other analysts, hoping together they could figure something out. Eventually, Barnes got wind of what they were doing and walked over to the desk where they were all working. Johnston tensed up a little as he approached. He made her a little nervous.

"What are you guys working on?"

"Oh, we're just trying to break a code," she answered.

"What kind of code?"

Johnston threw her arms up. "We don't know. That's what we're trying to figure out."

"Where'd it come from?"

"Oh, um, it was sent through a third-party source. They found it, didn't know what it was, so it wound up in our hands."

"Any guesses?"

She shook her head. "No, we're pretty stumped so far."

"What do you think it pertains to?"

Johnston took a deep breath. "Uh, I'm thinking it might have something to do with Europe, maybe? Or… Asia? It's tough to tell right now. It seems to be a pretty sophisticated code."

Barnes nodded, seeming satisfied with the answer. "Well, don't stay on it and neglect your other duties."

"Definitely not, sir."

He gently touched her arm, wanting her to walk over to the corner of the room with him so they could talk in private. He looked around to make sure nobody was in earshot.

"How are you getting along with the new agents?"

"Oh, very good," Johnston replied, putting her hands together in front of her chest as if she were praying. "The one operative is in the field. We're gathering some intel for him before he makes his move on his target. The other, we're waiting for clarification on something before we come up with a plan. Shouldn't take more than a day or two."

"Very good. You're doing good work."

"Thank you, sir."

Barnes looked around again. "What about Holt?"

Johnston took a deep breath, trying to say her words carefully. "He's... still thinking things over."

"Are you still on him?"

"Oh yes. I thought it'd be best to give him a little time after what happened. It was clear after our last conversation that he wasn't over his wife. You know, it's a shock, and he's clearly distraught. His mind is cloudy. I thought it'd be best to give him some time to work through that."

"Just don't let him slip away."

"I won't. I'll be in touch with him again very soon."

"We really could use him back. He'd be a great asset for us."

"I agree. I think once he's sorted through what he's going through, and his mind's clear... I'm confident we can reach him."

"Good. I'm counting on you."

"I'm doing my best, sir."

He touched her arm again. "Keep it up."

As Barnes walked away, Johnston wiped her forehead and exhaled. She didn't like being so secretive, but Holt asked her not to tell anyone. She wanted him to trust her. And if he was ever going to do that, she had to respect that. She could've gone back on her word, assuming that Holt would never find out, but that wasn't how she lived her life. She considered herself an honest person. She liked and respected people. If she gave her word to someone, regardless of the job she had, she had to follow through with it. Especially with someone like Holt.

"I can't keep doing this," she whispered.

Johnston went back to her desk and tried to work on a few things on her own. A couple of hours later, one of the analysts hit on something.

"Jo," an analyst shouted. "I think we've got something."

She hurried over to the desk with the others.

The analyst pointed to the computer screen, where a series of letters and numbers were displayed.

"Look at this," he said, his voice filled with excitement. "I ran the code through a different algorithm, and it seems to be revealing a message. At least part of one. We've only got the first part so far."

Johnston's eyes widened as she read the screen.

"White Horse... what? What's that mean?"

No one else could say. "That's all we've got so far. We'll keep trying to decipher."

"How much more is there?"

The analyst could only throw up his hands. "Uh, I

mean, looks like there's two or three more words. Maybe four."

"White Horse what? Is that a code name within the code?"

"Can't say yet?"

"Are you sure that's what it says?"

"Right now, I'm pretty sure it's accurate. Unless we come up with something else that changes it, but it seems pretty solid. System indicates it's a ninety percent match."

Johnston put her hand on her head and rubbed her forehead. "White Horse. A... code name. A bar. A restaurant. A tattoo? A nickname?"

Her mind raced with possibilities, trying to make sense of it. She knew that in the world of espionage, everything had a purpose. Very little, if anything, was random. She went back to her computer and brought up Holt's files. She typed in White Horse to see if anything popped up in connection with any of his past cases. The screen beeped. No match was found.

Johnston leaned back in her chair and sighed. They continued working on it for the next few hours, but they didn't get any closer to deciphering the rest of the code. As the hours ticked by, the frustration in the room only grew. They felt they were close, but still far apart at the same time.

Johnston felt a sense of urgency gnawing at her, wanting to solve the puzzle quickly before it slipped away from them. They had made progress with the first part of the message, but it wasn't enough. White Horse... what could it possibly mean? If they didn't solve it soon, depending on what it was, it might not mean much by the time they solved it. Whoever it was might have moved on, rendering the code meaningless.

Johnston's determination intensified as she delved deeper into her research. She scoured intelligence databases, cross-referencing the phrase "White Horse" with any relevant information she could find. She not only double-checked it against Holt's file again, but with anything that was known to the CIA. Her eyes grew strained as the night wore on, but she refused to give in to fatigue.

She was one of the few remaining members of the team left by that point. Almost everyone else had gone home. Johnston kept rubbing her eyes, knowing she was going to have to do the same soon. She was exhausted. But not only was she exhausted, she had exhausted all of her resources. White Horse didn't seem to apply to anything. At least nothing that they knew of just yet. As far as they knew, there were no missions, no targets, and no operatives with that code. It just wasn't on their radar yet.

Johnston powered off her computer. She was ready to call it a night. She didn't even know if White Horse applied to Holt's situation. It might have been something that didn't concern him at all. She'd take another stab at it in the morning. She wasn't giving up on it completely yet. At least they had White Horse. She'd let Holt know tomorrow. Maybe it would mean something to him. And maybe, she was one step closer to finally earning some trust.

9

Holt was still in Sicily, contemplating his next move. He was looking at his list of most likely suspects. He crossed off the names of Altmann and Pelligrini. His eyes glanced at the picture of Denise, which he had sitting on the table.

He started reminiscing about their life together. The laughter, the love, the memories. It felt like a lifetime ago, yet the pain was still fresh. As he stared at Denise's photo, a smile crept over his face. It was like he could see her in front of him. The way she laughed, the way she would crinkle her nose when she was teasing him, the warmth of her touch - all of it was a constant reminder of what he had lost. But it also fueled his determination for justice. For revenge.

His mind snapped back to the present, looking at his computer. He then hit a few keys, bringing up the picture of the man in the red hat. He stared at his photo for the next few minutes. Holt never wavered.

There was something about the man, an air of familiarity, that tugged at Holt's memory. But he just couldn't place where he had seen him before. Maybe he never had. But there was just something familiar about him, even though the face wasn't one that he could remember.

Holt closed his eyes and rubbed the bridge of his nose. He tried to relax his mind, shutting out all the turmoil that was running through it. Denise was clouding his thinking. He tried to think of only his former profession, almost trying to will this strange man into his thoughts, as if the answer would come to him at the snap of a finger.

Unfortunately, it wasn't that easy. No matter how hard he tried, no matter how long he strained his mind, the red-hatted man wasn't popping into his thoughts. Suddenly, his phone buzzed on the table, jolting him from his thoughts. He immediately picked it up. It was a message from Johnston.

"Hey. Think we might have something. Call me when you can."

Holt instantly dialed her back.

"Hey, that was quick. Figured I'd text you in case you were in the middle of something."

"I was just sitting here trying to figure things out."

"Get anywhere?"

Holt hesitated and sighed. "No. You said you had something?"

"We deciphered part of the code you sent."

"Part?"

"The first part. We believe it begins with White Horse."

"White Horse?"

"Yeah. We're still working on the rest of it. We're thinking there's another three or four words after it. Does that mean anything to you?"

Holt started thinking, trying to remember every case he'd ever been on. Every person he'd ever come across. Every building he'd ever been in. But nothing came to him.

"I went through your files," Johnston said. "I couldn't find any reference to a White Horse in them."

Holt still hesitated in his reply. "It doesn't sound familiar."

"I found some references to other cases, but they were wrapped up thirty years ago. I don't see any relevance to you. You don't remember anything?"

"Nothing that I recall."

"I mean, it is always possible that the code doesn't pertain to you at all. Could be something else entirely."

Holt was silent, what seemed like a million things crossing through his mind.

"Can I ask where you got the code?" Johnston asked.

Holt still wasn't sure if he should tell her. But then he figured if he told her, maybe that would help to decipher the rest of it. Maybe that would be the missing piece they needed. Maybe they could reference other things Pelligrini had written for them to match.

"An old contact of mine. I worked with him numerous times."

"Which one?"

Holt still had a paused response. "Giorgio Pelligrini."

Johnston instantly started typing. "Pelligrini. I remember seeing the name in your files. Wait a minute. If you got the code from Pelligrini, why can't you just ask him what it says? Can't you find him?"

"I did find him. He's dead."

"He's what?"

"Went to his house. Found him tied up, beaten up, and dead in the basement. Sitting in a chair."

Now it was Johnston's turn to be silent. "And the code?"

"Found it in his study on his desk under some papers."

"Do you know for sure this pertains to you?"

"No."

Johnston continued typing. "Pelligrini's in Sicily. Is that where you're at right now?"

"Yes."

"What are your plans right now?"

"I have a list of the most likely suspects. People who've sworn to come after me, or who know my name."

"Have you come across anyone else?"

"Detlef Altmann. I don't think he's involved."

Johnston quickly typed Altmann's name in, seeing the case file. "And why not?"

"I talked to him. I was satisfied with his answers."

Johnston tried to process everything she was hearing. "OK. It seems like a big coincidence that Pelligrini winds up dead not long after your wife does."

"His body was cold. He might've been killed before her."

"So what's your next step?"

"I don't know."

Johnston wasn't sure she believed him. "Aaron. Don't shut me out. I'm here. I'm helping you. I'm doing what you've asked. Either trust me and give me the whole story or do this on your own. Stop giving me bits and pieces. Give me everything or give me nothing. I can't operate only knowing half the story."

Holt leaned forward on the table in front of him, putting his hand on his head. His eyes went back to his computer screen, staring at the red-hatted man. He knew if he had any shot of identifying this man, he was probably going to have to put Johnston in the loop.

"There is something else."

Johnston stopped typing, hearing the gravity in his voice. "What is it?"

"There's a man. I don't know who he is. I know he was at my house the night Denise died."

"How do you know?"

"I had cameras set up around the perimeter of the place. I went back and checked all the footage and found this guy. He doesn't look like someone I've come across, though. It's not a great picture. Mostly the side of his face."

"It's something to work off of."

"I don't know if he's partially involved, like a lookout or something. Or if he's the one that..." Holt gulped. "Or if he's the one that actually pulled the trigger."

Johnston's heart ached for him. She closed her eyes for a moment. She could hear the pain in his voice. She wished she could ease the burden for him.

"Can I ask you something?"

"I don't recall you asking before."

Johnston chuckled. "Fair point. But if you think this guy is the one who killed Denise, why are you in Sicily checking out these other people?"

"Because I don't recognize this guy. And if I don't recognize him, that means I don't know him. I've never come across him before. Which means someone hired him to do it. Someone else was behind it."

"Is there any chance you might just be forgetting him?"

"I remember every face I've ever killed. I remember all the names. I might not remember every place or address. I might not know where they are right now. But I know the faces I've done business with. There's something familiar about him. But I don't know why. I figure it's unlikely I'll find this guy first. But maybe if I find the guy that hired him, then I'll find him."

"Can you send me the photo? I promise I'll be discreet. I can start working on it. Maybe between the picture, and Pelligrini, and the code, we can figure out what's going on."

Holt took a deep breath. "I would just like to, uh... thank you."

"Of course."

"I mean, I know you're only doing it to get me back into the fold, but..."

"That's not why I'm doing it," Johnston said.

"Really?"

"I know you think that's why. But it's not why."

"Then what is?"

Johnston wiped her eyes, getting emotional just thinking about it. "Because you're a man who's had his heart ripped away, and you're in pain. I just want to help you get through this and wind up on the other side."

"Why? You don't even know me."

"I don't know. I'd like to think I'm a good person that would do it for anybody. At least as much as I'm able to."

"You're, uh... you should think about looking for a new line of work."

The Nobody Man

"Why's that?"

"Because you're not cold-blooded and heartless enough for this job."

Johnston laughed. "Is that what you really think?"

"I think maybe if I knew you before I... anyway, um... there's another name I have to visit."

"OK. I'll see what I can come up with on the photo. And we'll keep working on the code."

"Thank you."

"Where will you be?"

Holt hesitated, not sure if he wanted to say. Normally, he wouldn't bother. But there was something about her that put him at ease. She had the type of personality that he gravitated to. She just seemed nice. It wasn't something he was used to in the profession.

"Monaco."

"What, or who, is there?" Johnston asked.

"A man named Gabriel Boucher."

"Boucher. I think I saw his name in your file."

"Worked with me on several jobs."

"And what's his significance?"

"It didn't end well with him."

Johnston scrunched her eyebrows together as she looked at Boucher's file. "I don't recall anything in the notes of a problem."

"Not everything makes it to those reports."

"So what was the issue?"

"My last assignment with him, I was there to take out one man."

"So what's the problem with that?"

"He wanted me to take out additional targets," Holt answered.

"Seems just like a difference of opinion. Hardly worth killing… taking revenge on you."

"I later learned that the people I chose not to kill… weeks later, killed some of his friends."

"OK. So maybe that is motivation for revenge."

"I don't know. I never heard any chatter about him looking for me, but… he knew my real name. It's worth checking out."

"OK. Can you do me a favor?"

"If I can."

"Can you just keep me in the loop about what you're doing and where you're going from now on? Not as a handler, or a CIA contact, or anything. Just as a friend. I would just feel better knowing where you are."

"As much as I can," Holt said.

"Thank you. I'll let you get going. I'll call you if I find out anything else. Good luck with your search."

"Thanks."

Holt hung up and put his phone down. He looked down at the table at the picture of Denise. He put his fingers on his face, as if he were stroking her face.

"I won't give up. Not until I find them."

10

Johnston was working at her desk. She was still trying to decipher the rest of the code. She was also trying to identify the man in the photo that Holt emailed to her. On another computer, she had Pelligrini's information pulled up. She also had various people coming up to her asking her questions, getting her feedback on a variety of topics. At times, it felt like her head was spinning.

She was just about to go to lunch. Then, her phone rang. She quickly looked at it, wondering what fire she was going to have to put out now. Her facial expression quickly changed when she saw it was her boyfriend, Jared, calling. She eagerly answered.

"Hey stranger."

"Hey. How's work?"

"Oh, you know... busy as always."

"So the reason I'm calling is... I was wondering if you wanted to have dinner tonight?"

"Of course," Johnson replied. "Where?"

"I was thinking about Lilly's."

"Lilly's? Really? Fancy. So what's the occasion?"

"I just thought me and my favorite girl could use a night out somewhere."

"We usually only go there for special occasions."

"Well, this will be a special occasion. You just have to wait and see what it is."

"Oh? No hints?"

"I think you're going to be very happy."

"So does this have to do with us?" Johnston asked.

"Maybe."

"Does it have to do with...?"

"No more hints. It just has to do with us and our future. And that's all I'm gonna say for now. The rest, you'll just have to hear in person."

"You're gonna keep me in suspense for the rest of the day, huh?"

"Yep. So I'll see you tonight? I'll pick you up at seven?"

"Sounds good. Love you."

"Love you too."

Johnston stared at her phone for a while after hanging up, thinking of all the possibilities. She was trying not to let her mind run wild. But she was getting a little nervous thinking about what she hoped it was.

They'd been together for about two years and three months, and they'd seen each other on a few dates before becoming official for about a month before that. Johnston had dropped numerous hints over the past couple of months about maybe taking the next step in their relationship.

Right now, they lived in separate apartments. She was hoping he would propose soon, then they could move in together before getting married. Jared was a lawyer for a smaller firm in the area, but he was putting out feelers, and interviewing for various law firms across the country. Bigger firms. More prestigious. More money.

As Johnston continued to daydream about what the special occasion could be, a sudden jolt of excitement surged through her. What if Jared really was going to propose tonight? The thought made her heart race with anticipation. She had been ready for this moment for a while now, and the idea that it might finally happen filled her with joy.

Johnston walked out of the building, and headed to a small outdoor cafe that she liked to frequent. She called her best friend, Gianna.

"Hey, what's up?"

Johnston was beaming. "Jared's taking me to Lilly's tonight."

"Really? What's the occasion?"

"I don't know. It has to be something big, right?"

"You don't think tonight's the night, do you?"

Johnston couldn't stop smiling. "I don't know. I don't want to get ahead of myself and get disappointed if it's not. But I keep thinking about it."

"What else could it be? It's not your birthday, anniversary, what else is there?"

"Nothing. That I know of. Do you really think this might be it?"

"Well, what'd he say?"

"He said this will be a special occasion, and that I'll be very happy, and that it has to do with us and our future."

"Oh my gosh, it sounds like he's going to pop the question."

"I know, right? But I'm trying not to let my mind race ahead, you know? Just in case."

"What else could it be?"

"I don't know of anything else."

"Oh my gosh, I'm so excited. You're going to have to tell me all about it when you get home. Well, unless you have a little celebration afterwards. Then maybe tomorrow."

"I'll call you as soon as I'm done."

Johnstone hung up and ate her lunch, which consisted of a salad, most of which she picked at. She was too excited to eat. After she was done, she headed back to the office.

Once there, she sat back down at her desk, trying

to refocus. She had a hard time containing her excitement. Thoughts of the upcoming dinner with Jared and the tantalizing possibility of a future together filled her mind. She couldn't help but imagine what it would be like to wake up every morning next to him, to build a life together, and to start a family someday. It was the kind of happiness she had always dreamed of.

But amidst her excitement, there was also a nagging feeling of unease. She glanced at her computer screens, the mysterious code, Pelligrini, and the photo of the man in the red hat came back to the forefront of her mind. She knew she couldn't afford to let her mind become distracted. Not while Holt was still out there trying to find his wife's killer.

Another analyst walked over to Johnston's desk. He would have disappointing news to share.

"Facial scans on that guy are coming up empty."

"Not even a partial?" Johnston asked.

The analyst shook his head. "Nah. His head's turned in a way, along with the hat, and it's dark... it's just not a great photo."

Johnston leaned back in her chair, nodding along, staring at her computer screens while she picked at her lip with her finger. There was something there. Something they weren't seeing. There had to be. This couldn't all be a dead end, or a coincidence. Something had to fit together.

"What about the code?"

"Still trying to break it. All we have so far is the White Horse. Not really any closer yet."

Johnston lowered her head and put her hands on her hair. She alternated tapping on her head with her fingers of both hands as she thought. She went back to the photo, trying to enhance it, bringing up different angles. None of it seemed to make a difference. Her eyes went back to the logo on the front of the hat.

She pointed to it. "What's that logo?"

"We haven't been able to make it out yet."

Johnston leaned in closer, zooming in on the photo, squinting her eyes, desperately wanting, needing to find something.

"It almost looks like an X."

"Yeah, but that could be just about anything. Or nothing."

Johnston zoomed in on it even more. Though it was becoming more distorted, she used a program to try to clean it up. She pointed to it again.

"Look, the lines aren't straight. They angle slightly. Almost the way lightning bolts do, you know?"

"Yeah, I can see that."

"And look, is that another image? Like the outline of it?"

"I mean, it could be. It's just so hard to tell."

"I'll keep working on it."

As the analyst went back to his desk, Johnston went into the CIA's database of all known logos. She typed in an X, and started making her way through it all. And there were thousands upon thousands of images.

She sighed. "This is gonna take a while."

She was hoping that somewhere in this database lied the answer. If she could find that logo, that might have been the key to unlocking this entire mystery. It didn't look like a regular hat and logo that was bought at your local department store. This looked like a custom design. Something that could be identified if she could just find something to compare it to.

After hours of searching and countless cups of coffee, Johnston was starting to lose hope. The logo remained elusive, blending into a vast sea of other images in the database. She rubbed her temples, feeling the exhaustion creeping in.

But she refused to give up. She knew that if she could just find a match, it might lead her one step closer to uncovering the truth. It had to be there. It just had to be. She continued looking.

Finally, after a few more hours of searching, she found something. The logo she was looking at bore a striking resemblance to the one on the hat. At least the parts she could see. The database had an X, with the lightning bolt lines crossing. It looked identical. The database also had a skull in the middle of the X where the lines intersected. She looked back at the photo. It might've been a match. She couldn't see the entire image, but there definitely was the outline of one. It could have been a skull.

Armed with new hope and excitement, Johnston saw the logo in the database belonged to a group called The Black Phoenix. It wasn't a group she was familiar with. She quickly typed in The Black Phoenix to get a rundown on them. As soon as the results popped up, she glanced over at the time, realizing she had lost track of it.

"Oh, shoot, I gotta go."

Before delving too deep into the rabbit hole that would cause her to miss her dinner, she wrote some notes to herself so she'd know where to pick back up when she came back in the morning.

She stood up, looking down at her computer, feeling guilty about leaving when she felt like she was so close to getting some answers. Well, hopefully getting some answers. There was no guarantee this would lead anywhere either.

She remained standing there, thinking about her boyfriend, wondering if she should cancel to keep pursuing what The Black Phoenix meant. Holt was desperate for some answers. But she also didn't know if this was going to provide any. There might not have been any relation at all.

Johnston felt the pull in both directions. They both seemed to be crying for her attention. She thought about Holt, and how he was probably on a plane to Monaco right now, anyway. Or just getting off of it. He was still pursuing his leads. He wasn't out there with nothing. She could afford to take a night off for herself. She talked herself into keeping her dinner plans.

She pointed at her computer, as if it could hear her talking to it. "Tomorrow... I'm gonna get to the bottom of this. I'm gonna get to the bottom of what this is all about. You and me... we're gonna do this."

11

After leaving the office, Johnston hurried back to her apartment so she could get ready for dinner. She wanted to look her best for the special occasion, so she chose a black dress that accentuated her figure, with spaghetti straps, and a plunging neckline, with the dress going down to her knees to match her favorite pair of heels. She sat in front of her mirror and applied some makeup, which she didn't do often.

Her attire for work mostly consisted of dress pants and a blouse, sometimes alternating between heels or flat shoes. She just finished getting ready when she heard the doorbell. She hurried over to it and opened the door, seeing her boyfriend standing there in a nice suit. She hugged him, and planted a kiss on his lips.

"You look amazing."

Johnston smiled, appreciative of the compliment. "Thank you."

"Are you ready?"

"Yep. Just let me get my purse."

As they drove to the restaurant, Johnston started getting butterflies in her stomach. She was trying to keep herself under control, but it was hard to do at the moment. She could feel her hands clamming up.

Once they reached the restaurant and went inside, Johnston's heart pounded with anticipation. The ambiance was perfect for a romantic dinner, with jazz music playing in the background. There was soft lighting overhead, and a flickering candlelight illuminating each table. The maitre d' led them to a private booth in the back of the restaurant, secluded from the rest of the diners.

Jared pulled out the chair for her and she gracefully sat down, her excitement bubbling beneath her calm exterior. The waiter arrived, presenting them with menus and taking their drink orders. They both ordered a glass of wine.

Johnston glanced at the menu distractedly, her mind preoccupied with what might unfold tonight. Jared reached across the table, gently taking her hand in his.

"You look beautiful," he told her.

"Thank you. You look very handsome, too."

"I can't wait to spend the rest of our lives together."

"Me too."

Her heart skipped a beat. She swallowed nervously, feeling a mix of emotions, though it was all happy thoughts. She was just waiting for the moment. She nervously twitched with her hands, wondering if this was going to be it. She glanced around the room, anxiously waiting.

"You know, I did bring you here for a reason," Jared said.

"Oh? What reason is that?"

"Well, this is our place. This is where we've gone for every major thing. Valentine's Day. Our first and second anniversary of dating. This seemed like the right place for the next part of our lives."

Johnston tried to contain her smile, though she was failing miserably at it. She was waiting for her boyfriend to get out of his chair and drop to a knee next to the table.

"I guess there's really no easy way to do this."

Johnston gulped. She had no words, anticipating what was about to happen.

"I'll just come out with it." Jared had a big smile on his face, but he made no move to get out of his chair. "I got it."

"What?"

"I got the job. They called me this morning."

The smile slowly faded from Johnston's face, though she did a good job of trying to keep it plastered on to hide her disappointment.

"Oh. Well... that's great. That's... really great. I'm so happy for you."

Jared took a sip of his wine. "Thank you. I was so

nervous. I wasn't sure they were going to offer it to me. It's such a weight off my mind."

"Yeah, mine too."

"Isn't this the best news?"

She tried to keep an upbeat face. "Yeah. Yeah, it really is. So, uh, is that the only reason we're here tonight?"

"Of course, what else would there be?"

"Oh, nothing. Nothing I can think of. I just wanted to make sure you weren't going to spring some other wonderful news on me."

Jared put his hand on hers. She didn't pull it away, though she really wanted to.

"This is enough big news for one day, don't you think?"

Johnston nervously laughed. "Yeah. Yeah, it is."

She felt like such a fool right now for believing that he might pop the question to her. All that nervous energy she had was forming into something else. Something not as pleasant.

"I know you have two or three months left on the lease to your apartment, right?"

"About that."

"It'll suck to pay for an empty apartment for a month or two, but it'll be worth it, right?"

Johnston looked confused. "What are you talking about?"

"Your apartment. You're coming with me, right?"

Her mouth fell open, and she licked her lips. She

shook her head, trying to get things right in her mind. She slid her hand out from under his.

"Coming with you? Did you already accept this job?"

"Well of course I did. It's a great opportunity. Why wouldn't I?"

A lump went down her throat. "Um, maybe because you didn't discuss it with me first."

"What's there to discuss? You knew I interviewed for it. You knew I wanted it."

"Yes, and I thought before you accepted it... I just assumed you'd discuss it with me first. You know, so we can figure out what it means for us?"

"Nothing has to change between us. I just assumed you'd come out there with me."

"Come out there with you? How exactly is that going to work?"

"Well I don't want to do the long-distance thing. I just figured you'd quit your job here and find something out there."

Johnston raised an eyebrow. "You expected me to quit my job and just follow you out there?"

"Well, yeah, why not?"

"Because my work is here, my job is here, I have family nearby. Friends. I'm getting more responsibilities, I'm... getting somewhere here."

"Can't you just transfer out there?"

"You know there's no CIA building in California."

"I thought you could just transfer to the FBI or something. That's possible, right?"

Johnston's head was swimming. "Uh, yeah, yeah, I guess so. But I don't want to work for the FBI. I'm happy doing what I'm doing. And besides, that's a complex process to transfer."

"I thought you'd be happy for me."

"Um, I am. I'm just... this wasn't what I thought I was going to hear. It's kind of just thrown at me."

"We've always talked of taking the next step."

"Yeah. Here. Not in California. I don't have a life out there."

"We could make one. Together."

Johnston took a sip of her wine. "And when do you go out there? Do you know yet?"

Jared kept smiling. "They want me out there within the month. Isn't that great?"

Johnston couldn't even fake a smile anymore. "Yeah. Really great."

"What's the matter?"

"Because you just accepted this job without even talking to me about it. And then you just assumed I'd follow you out there without a second thought. Like I have nothing else worthy in my life except following you around."

"Jo, we talked about this."

"No, we didn't. Not this. I'm supposed to just drop everything in my life here and follow you without even a discussion?"

"This is a great job for me. Almost four times my current salary. This is a big break."

"Yeah, and that's nice for you. But I don't see how this works for us."

Jared leaned back in his seat, frustrated that his girlfriend was making a big deal out of it.

"Why do you have to be doing this right now?"

Johnston just shook her head at his lack of self-awareness. "Why do *I* have to be doing this? Do you not even see?"

"See what? I see a great opportunity."

"For you."

"For us. Why don't you see that?"

Johnston stood up, ready to leave. "All I can see is that you're only considering yourself and what's best for you. And that's got nothing to do with us."

"Where are you going?"

"Home."

She started walking away.

"How are you going to get there?"

"I'll call a cab."

As Johnston walked toward the exit, she took out her phone from her purse. She called Gianna.

"You're calling me already, did it really happen?!"

Johnston fought back tears. "Gi, can you come pick me up?"

Gianna could hear how upset her friend was. "Of course. What happened? Did he not ask?"

"No, he didn't. And it's a complete disaster."

"Oh, no. What happened?"

"He got a new job and is moving away, and he apparently just expects me to follow him."

"Are you serious?" Gianna asked.

"Yeah. I'll tell you everything. Can you get me?"

"Yeah, I'll be there in twenty minutes."

"Thanks."

"Just stay there. I'm on my way."

"Hope you have plenty of alcohol at your place right now," Johnston said.

"Trust me, I do."

"Good. I'm gonna need it."

12

After the five-hour flight to Monaco, Holt went straight for his target. With only around 35,000 inhabitants, Monaco is the second smallest country in the world. It's located on the northern coast of the Mediterranean Sea, bordered by France and Italy.

Tourism is one of Monaco's main sources of income, and gambling and casinos were also right at the heart of it. Gabriel Boucher was head of security at one of the casinos. It was a lucrative job, and Holt knew from their past interactions, the man wasn't leaving that job unless he was fired or killed. And considering how good he was at the former, that wasn't happening.

Armed with an expensive-looking suit, blending in with the high-rollers, Holt entered the casino. He instantly started looking around. He made his way to a few slot machines, played a few rounds of blackjack, and even went to the roulette table. He did this for about an hour, mostly scanning the room in the hopes of getting a glimpse of Boucher.

Holt won a few hundred, then lost a few hundred, and in the end, came out just about even. He wasn't really concentrating much. Even if he was, he was never much of a gambler. He just didn't care for it enough. He'd seen way too many people get addicted and get into trouble over it.

After leaving the roulette table, Holt meandered around the floor. It was always possible Boucher was off. Or maybe he was watching the cameras from the security room. But Holt would give it some more time. From his previous time with Boucher, he knew the security boss liked to roam the floor from time to time. Boucher always said you couldn't see everything from a camera. Sometimes, you just needed to see things with your own eyes.

With that knowledge, Holt hoped he just needed to wait long enough for Boucher to make an appearance. As Holt continued to wander through the casino, he glanced at his watch. It had been over two hours since he arrived, and there was still no sign of Gabriel Boucher. He started to wonder how much more time he was going to give it. Not that he had anywhere else to be at the moment.

Just as doubt began to creep in, a commotion erupted at one of the blackjack tables. A man, tall and imposing, stood up from his seat and started shouting at the dealer.

"You're cheating me! I know it!" the man shouted, slamming his fist onto the table.

The dealer, clearly taken aback by the sudden outburst, stammered in response. "Sir, I assure you, everything is on the up-and-up."

Holt swiftly made his way toward the chaos, discreetly blending in with the crowd that had gathered around. The man's face was contorted with anger, his voice carrying above the murmurs of onlookers. Suddenly, another man knifed his way through the crowd. He had an impeccably tailored suit on, with an earpiece in, and slicked-back black hair, that was slightly receding. It was Gabriel Boucher. There were two other muscular gentlemen right behind him, no doubt colleagues.

Boucher went straight up to the man with the issue, and put his hand on his arm to try to settle him down. Boucher talked calmly at first, and while it seemed to work in the beginning, the man still insisted he was being cheated. Boucher only had so much patience. He would try the easy way at first. But he wouldn't try it for long. He'd try it for a few minutes, but that was it.

Boucher, sensing the argument wasn't going anywhere, looked to the two men that worked with him. He gave them a slight nod of his head, which was all the sign they needed. They went over to the man and grabbed each of his arms, barely picking the man off the floor. They escorted the man to the door.

Boucher turned to look at the gathering crowd. He smiled at them.

"The casino offers its apologies for the intrusion. As a token of our appreciation for your patronage, we would like to offer everyone a free ten dollar chip on the house."

The offer received a round of applause from the crowd.

Boucher smiled. "Good luck to you all."

Boucher started to walk away. Holt followed, though he wasn't particularly close. Boucher never noticed him.

"Very generous of you," Holt said.

Boucher stopped in his tracks. He never turned around. He stared straight ahead. It wasn't much of a sample, but he knew that voice. But he hadn't heard it in a long time. Holt continued walking towards him.

"Let other people do your dirty work now for you, do you?"

Boucher still remained stationed to the floor, not moving an inch. He was trying to collect his thoughts. Finally, he swiftly turned around. The two men stood there, staring at each other. Boucher's eyes narrowed as he scrutinized Holt, barely believing the man was really standing there in front of him. The two men stood there in a tense silence, the casino patrons blissfully unaware as they walked past. Finally, a small grin emerged on Boucher's face.

"Is it really you?"

"As far as I can tell," Holt replied.

"What are you doing here?"

"Just figured I'd catch up with an old friend."

"It's been a long time."

"Yeah, it sure has."

Boucher took a quick look around, seeing his two companions coming back. He put his finger up to Holt to give him a second as he went over to the other two men to give them instructions while he was off duty. After he was finished, he waved at Holt to follow him over to the bar. They went over to a table, and Boucher waved for a small bottle and a couple of glasses.

"So what brings you here?" Boucher asked. "On the job?"

"In a way."

A waitress brought the bottle and glasses over, setting them down on the table.

"I assume you're not here to reminisce," Boucher said, pouring their drinks.

Holt picked his up and took a sip. "Looking for someone."

"That kind of goes without saying, doesn't it?"

"It's personal to me."

Boucher took a big gulp of his. "Seems like you're beating around the bush here, Aaron. It's not really your style. Why don't you just come out with it?"

The Nobody Man

Holt had his hands around his glass, spinning it around. "Someone killed my wife."

Boucher froze, not moving a muscle, not even twitching, as he processed what he just heard. His facial expression was a mix of shock, uncertainty, and a little fear. He finally moved, looking down for a moment.

"I'm sorry to hear that. Why does that bring you here, though?"

"One of my last missions was with you," Holt said. "As I recall, it didn't end well between us."

"That was just business."

"You thought I should've gone further."

"Still do."

"Other people got killed."

"Shouldn't have happened."

"And you said you'd get even with me."

Boucher scoffed, putting his hands up. "Look, I was frustrated. You know that. Sometimes you say things in the heat of the moment that you don't mean. I'm sure you've done it. We all have. That doesn't mean I'd follow through with it."

Holt sat there, quietly, analyzing his former associate.

"Wait a minute, Aaron, you think I'd come after you after all this time? Three years? C'mon. Why would I do that?"

"To make it seem like it wasn't you?"

"Come on, be reasonable. I don't even know where

you live."

"You know my name. Finding my address wouldn't be too much of a stretch for someone like you."

"Aaron, come on. I like you. We always got along. So we had a difference of opinion on a job, so what? It happens. I'm not gonna go kill your family over it. And believe me, I wouldn't kill your wife and leave you breathing, that's for sure. I've seen you work. I know what you're capable of. I wouldn't kill your wife just so you could hunt me down. And I sure as hell wouldn't be standing right here in a place you know and could find me."

"What do you know about White Horse?" Holt asked.

"White Horse? What is that?"

Holt shrugged. "You tell me."

Boucher shook his body, as if he were searching for an answer. "I couldn't tell you. Never heard of it before. What is it?"

"Part of a message I found. Thought it might be a code name or something."

Boucher shook his head. "Nothing I've ever heard before."

Holt continued staring at him. He thought Boucher was telling the truth. His body relaxed, and he leaned back, taking another sip of his drink. Boucher noticed his friend's relaxed posture and took a sigh of relief. Though Boucher was a tough guy in his own right, he knew he was nothing compared to Holt. The Nobody

Man was on another level. He knew Holt could kill in more ways than any person should know. Boucher had no problem arguing or debating with him, but he sure didn't want Holt for an enemy. No chance of that.

"Look, I'm sorry about your wife. I am. But if you think I had anything to do with it, you came a very long way for nothing."

Holt reached into his pocket and removed a picture. He slid it along the table. "Ever see this guy before?"

Boucher picked up the picture of the man in the red hat, studying it closely. After a minute or two, he shook his head.

"No, I'm afraid I don't. Who is he?"

"He was there the night my wife was killed."

Boucher took another look at the photo, squinting his eyes. "What's that on his hat?"

"Some type of logo. Haven't figured it out yet. Recognize it?"

"No, I don't think so." Boucher slid the photo back to him. "Wish I could help you. I really do."

Holt took the picture back and put it in his pocket. "You already have."

"Yeah? How you figure that?"

"Well, if I can't find the person who did it, then I'll cross off the people that I know didn't. If I cross off enough names, eventually, there'll only be one left."

"Process of elimination."

Holt nodded. "Yeah."

"What do you plan to do with this guy when you find him?"

Holt gave him an eye, as if he really needed to explain. "I think you already know the answer to that one."

"I'd hate to be that guy when you find him."

"So will he."

13

Just a few minutes after Holt stepped foot into his hotel room, his phone rang. It was Johnston. It was a video call. He answered, going over to the kitchen table and sitting down to talk.

"Yeah?"

"You look beat," Johnston said.

"Nah, not really."

"How's Monaco?"

"Uneventful."

"No answers?"

"Not the ones I was looking for."

Johnston continued talking, but Holt wasn't really listening. He was staring at her face. There was something different about her. She had more makeup on. Much more than the other times he'd seen her. After a minute, Johnston realized he didn't hear a word she was saying.

"Are you listening to me?"

"What?"

Johnston's shoulders slumped. "Are you tuning me out?"

"Oh, no, I'm sorry, it's not that."

"Then what is it?"

"What's wrong with you?"

Johnston's head snapped back. "Excuse me?"

"You have a lot more makeup on. Like you're hiding something."

"I'm not hiding anything."

"Is there something wrong?"

"No, nothing's wrong. I just felt like wearing more makeup today. Is that OK with you?"

Holt shrugged. "I guess. Just thought something was wrong."

"Well, nothing's wrong."

"Just thought there was. I mean, you want me to be honest and trust you, so I thought maybe you should do the same."

"That's got nothing to do with this."

"Then what's it got to do with?"

"It's... nothing. You and I are business, and this is... this is just... nothing."

"Sounds like it's something."

"It's, uh, um... well... I don't, uh... I'm not doing this."

"Sure sounds like something."

"It's just a personal thing. It has nothing to do with

you."

"I'm just saying. If you want me to trust you, then you should trust me."

"I don't even believe we're having this conversation. My personal business has nothing to do with you."

"Oh, but my personal business you get to invade?" Holt shook his head. "Not how it works, Josie."

"Josie?"

Holt hit the red button and hung up. Johnston's eyes widened, realizing he ended their conversation.

"You just hung up on me. And you called me Josie? Nobody calls me Josie."

She immediately redialed Holt's number. He let it ring a few times before answering.

"You hung up on me."

Holt grinned. "Sorry. Finger slipped."

"Right. And don't call me Josie."

"Why not?"

"No one's ever called me Josie."

"So what does everyone call you?" Holt asked.

"Jo. Most people call me Jo."

Holt grimaced. "Eh, I don't know about that. You don't look like a Jo to me."

"Seriously?"

"You look more like a Josie. It's a prettier name. More fitting for you."

Johnston opened her mouth, as if she were going to keep debating. Then she thought against it. He just complimented her. It felt like they were making progress in their relationship. She'd take the small victories when she could get them.

"So..." she hesitated. "I lost my train of thought."

"You were telling me what's wrong."

"I was not."

"Then we have nothing else to talk about."

Holt hung up again. Johnston prided herself on keeping a level head. She wasn't one to get angry very often, other than boyfriends who had their heads up their ass. She was usually a very happy person. But she was starting to get a little angry here. She waited a minute to try to calm down before calling Holt back for a third time.

"Do not hang up on me again."

"You sound a little mad," Holt said.

Johnston looked around to make sure no one was watching. She tried to keep her voice down.

"Yes, because you keep hanging up on me!"

"Because you won't trust me."

"I do trust you. I trust you enough to not tell anyone what you're doing right now."

"So tell me what's bothering you so we can move on. I'm not doing anything else until you do."

"Why is this so important to you?"

Holt sighed, trying to measure his words carefully. "This is all about that trust thing. I don't trust many people. I still don't trust you completely."

"Why not? What else can I do for you?"

"Open up. Be a real person. Right now, you're just a

suit in an agency that I know will lie to me any chance it gets to bring me in. As far as I'm concerned, you're just a byproduct of that. I want to know the person that I'm dealing with... there's a beating heart under that suit. There's a soul. It's not just some mindless robot that will say or do anything to make me believe they're with me even if they're not."

Johnston stared at him for a few seconds. She licked her lips. She was processing his words. She understood him. She could now see why he was so inquisitive. Trust was big for him. As he mentioned, he wanted to make sure she was a real person. She got it. Someone like him, that did the things he did, that took the risks he took, he couldn't afford to not trust people. That still didn't make it any easier to talk about, though. She took a deep breath.

She looked down for a moment. "I, uh... had a fight with my boyfriend last night."

"How long have you been together?"

"A little over two years."

"Bad?"

"I was crying all night."

Holt could see the emotion in her eyes. "Gonna be able to work it out?"

Johnston shook her head. "I don't know. He got a new job out in California. Just accepted it without discussing it with me first. Without any regard for us. He just expects me to quit my job and move out there with him."

"What would you do out there?"

Johnston shrugged. "I don't know. He mentioned me transferring to the FBI or something."

"Good work."

"But my heart is here. My work. My friends. My family. And he didn't consider any of it. He just..."

"Only thought about himself."

"Yeah. At least that's my point of view. I'm sure he feels differently."

"So when does the new job start?"

"A few weeks."

"Want some relationship advice from someone who's been there?"

"Sure."

"You both have to be willing to sacrifice and compromise for the other. If you're both not willing to do that, you've only got one side trying to make it work. And that's a relationship that's doomed to fail."

Johnston smiled. "Maybe you should think about writing a relationship column. Seems like you have good advice."

Holt grinned. "Maybe my next career."

As Holt looked at her, he could tell her mind was wandering. Probably thinking about her boyfriend. He felt badly that he made her open up and relive it again, but he did need to make sure that he was right about her. He had her pegged as someone who was nice and friendly, but also loyal. He had a good feeling about her.

But if she wasn't willing to open up to him, he couldn't trust her completely. And it wasn't just her. It was anyone he worked with. He had to know as much about them as he could. Their past, their thoughts, their future plans and goals, what made them tick, everything. He needed to know if there was something that would make him think twice about them, or make sure his back wasn't turned completely towards them. He had to know they were with him. He was beginning to feel like Johnston was.

"So what were you saying before we got sidetracked?" Holt asked.

"Well that was your fault!"

Holt smiled. "Guilty."

"Anyway, um... what was I saying? Oh yes, I'm thinking we're going about this completely wrong. Well, at the risk of pissing you off, I think you're going about this completely wrong."

"Oh? How so?"

Johnston took a deep breath, not wanting to make him mad with what she was about to say. "You're just flying from place to place, going after people on a whim, and talking to people in your former life."

"And that's a problem?"

"That's not the solution. You're just spinning your wheels. You need a better plan. Respectfully."

"And you have one?" Holt said, crossing his arms.

"Well, I mean, look. You're going after people who know your real name, right?"

"Seems to be a good place to start."

"But it's backwards. It doesn't make sense. If someone knew your real name, they wouldn't take three years to do this. If they had a grudge, they would've found you long before now. And they wouldn't let you live for you to come back after them."

"So you think it's someone who didn't know my name?"

"Not until recently," Johnston answered. "This was something that just got leaked to them, or they just found out. And I'm thinking it's retaliation for something you did."

"Such as?"

"I don't know. But whoever killed your wife, they could've waited around for you. But they didn't. You weren't their target. They wanted to kill your wife to make you suffer. Probably because they have suffered. You took something from them. They wanted to return the favor."

"The wife or husband of someone I killed."

Johnston nodded. "That's what I'm thinking."

Holt sat there thinking about it. "Could be."

Johnston nervously gulped, a little worried at talking to him so forcefully. "Hopefully you take my opinion in the spirit in which it was given."

Holt looked away from the screen, giving it some thought. "Makes sense."

"It does?"

"So what do you think my next move should be?"

Johnston looked surprised at the question. She really didn't expect to hear him deferring to her on it.

"Oh, um, well, you know... I'm also thinking that maybe Pelligrini was involved somehow. Either he sold you out and gave up your name after getting beaten, hence the way you found him, or he knew someone was after you, and he was tortured and killed to keep him from telling you that they were coming."

"But that code doesn't seem to mean anything."

"Not yet. I'm still working on it. And that reminds me, I found something else interesting." Johnston grabbed the picture off her desk of the man in the red hat. She held it up and pointed to the logo so Holt could see what she was referring to. "And I think I've identified this logo. It's an X, with the lightning bolts for lines, with a skull in the middle of it."

Holt took a gulp. "The Black Phoenix."

"What? You know?"

"I've heard of the group before."

"Really? What are they?"

"Basically, an international group of assassins. They sell themselves out to the highest bidder. They don't work for any particular country. They'll take out anybody if the price is right. And they aren't cheap. We're talking millions of dollars to hire them."

Johnston clasped her hands. "This is great. We've got a place to start. So now we know the group behind this."

"They don't work on their own. Someone hired them."

"That's OK. We can run down some names."

"As far as I know, there are no names. Nobody knows who is associated with them. They're a ghost organization. You don't find them. They find you."

"Well, as nice as that is to believe, it's a fairy tale. Someone knows how to find them. They don't just appear out of thin air. Someone has to be the frontman to hire them. And that's the one we have to find."

A solemn look appeared on Holt's face. If The Black Phoenix was involved, he knew his job became infinitely harder. Nobody knew how many people were even involved with The Black Phoenix. They were just as secretive as The Nobody Man was. But Holt was intent on finding out. Someone found him. Now it was his turn to flip the tables.

14

Johnston was on her lunch break, sitting at an outdoor cafe with Gianna. They were both eating a salad.

"So how's work?"

Johnston shrugged. "The usual."

"Anything fun popping up?"

"You know I can't talk about it."

"It's just us."

Johnston laughed. "And you know I still can't talk about it."

"Who's gonna know?"

"I'll know. Besides, they probably have this table bugged to trip up people that come here."

Gianna leaned to her left as if she were about to look under the table. "Really?"

"No, not really. But I still can't talk about it. You should know by now."

"Yeah, yeah. What about Jared? Heard from him?"

"Not since dinner the other night."

"What are you going to do?"

Johnston sighed. "I guess it's really up to him."

"What do you mean?"

"Whether he intends to take this new job or not."

"You're not gonna go out there with him."

Johnston shook her head. "No. It's, uh, I... I just can't. My life is here. And the way he presented it to me. It was just like he expected me to drop everything here and just follow him like a lost puppy. I mean, that's not how I thought our relationship was. I thought I loved him. We were together for two years."

"Were?"

"We've both made our positions clear. He doesn't want a long-distance relationship. I'm not willing to drop everything to move out there. That pretty much settles it, doesn't it?" She then thought back to what Holt told her. "Both sides have to be willing to sacrifice and compromise for the other. And I'm not sure either of us are."

Gianna's eyes got bigger as she looked past her friend at the man walking towards them. It was Jared. He knew Johnston liked to eat at that cafe at least three days a week.

"Um, I think I have to get back to work."

Johnston knew her friend still had time. "What? Why?"

She then turned around to see what had her so

The Nobody Man

flabbergasted. Gianna closed the lid to the box her salad was in, and got up.

"I'll call you later."

Johnston forced a smile. She went back to eating her food while she waited for her boyfriend to get there. As Gianna passed Jared, she smiled and waved at him. Once Jared arrived at the table, he pulled the chair out.

"Mind if I sit?"

Johnston lifted her hands, honestly not really caring. "If you want."

"You haven't answered any of my calls," Jared said, sitting down.

"I didn't really think we had much to talk about."

"C'mon, Jo. We can't do this. We have to figure this out. We can't just bury our heads and run away from it."

"That's not what I'm doing."

"Then what do you call it?"

Johnston hesitated. Maybe it was what she was doing. But she wasn't going to admit it.

"Uh... just... anyway, what are you doing here?"

"Wanted to talk to you. I mean, I'm leaving in two weeks. I want us to be good."

"So you're still leaving?"

"I already told you I accepted the position."

"Then I don't think we really have anything else to talk about," Johnston said.

"C'mon, Jo, you're really willing to throw away the last two years?"

"Why not? You did."

"That's not fair. I want you to come."

"You want me to come on your terms. Not on our terms. And you don't even see the difference. That's the point."

"No, I guess I don't see it. What's the problem?"

"Because this is all about you. Not us. If my job came to me and offered me a position in Paris, I wouldn't just instantly accept. I'd come home and talk to you about it and see if that worked for us. Whether you could get a job out there, whether you'd be willing to move out there, whether we could still make it work out there. I wouldn't just blindly say yes without discussing it with you."

"And if I said no?"

"Then I probably wouldn't take it," Johnston said. "If our relationship meant that much to me, I'd consider your feelings first. That's the difference between us."

Jared leaned back in his chair. "So you're saying this is it for us?"

"Yeah, I guess so."

"There's nothing else I can say or do?"

Johnston shook her head. "I don't think so."

Jared leaned forward. "Jo, I mean, what do you want me to do?"

"You've already decided what you wanted. You want that job. And that's fine. I'm not begrudging you for wanting a better opportunity. It's just that opportunity doesn't include me."

Jared put his hand over his mouth, trying to think of a way to salvage their relationship. "I want both."

Johnston sighed. "Look, we're both still young. We're trying to establish our careers. And our careers are taking us to two different places. You can pack up and move. I can't. And you were right, the long-distance thing probably won't work."

"What if I turn the job down?"

"You can't. You were excited enough to accept it in the first place. That's what you really wanted. And if you turn it down now, you're always going to resent me for keeping you here. Especially if a few years go by and you don't get a better opportunity at least equal to what you turned down. You're always going to wonder 'what if'? And I don't want to hold you back."

Jared looked around, taking a deep breath. It seemed as if there was nothing he could say or do to convince her their relationship could be saved. He felt a sinking feeling in his chest as he realized that she had her mind made up. He stared at Johnston, his heart heavy with the weight of their crumbling relationship.

They sat in silence for a few moments, their hearts heavy with the weight of their impending separation.

The bustling sounds of the cafe seemed distant and insignificant compared to the turmoil within their hearts.

Finally, Jared broke the silence. "I guess this is goodbye, then."

Johnston nodded, tears welling up in her eyes. "Yeah. I guess so."

They exchanged one last look before Jared rose from his seat. He stood there, staring at her, not really wanting to tear himself away.

"Maybe I'll call you before I leave?"

Johnston looked down at the table. "I don't think that'd be a good idea."

He wanted to reach out and put his hand on hers, but decided against it. It seemed as if her mind was made up. There was nothing else he could say to change it. He walked away, defeated.

Johnston continued looking down, picking at her salad. She didn't want to turn and watch him leave. That would indicate she still had mixed feelings. And she didn't. She knew this was the way it had to be. There was no looking back.

She put her fork down, and leaned her head on her fist, her elbow resting on the table. She just stared at her food, no longer interested in eating it. Her stomach was in knots. Even though she believed it was the right decision, it wasn't easy walking away from two years.

Her phone then rang. She sluggishly grabbed it out

of her purse, assuming it was Gianna. She was surprised to see it was an analyst from work.

"Johnston."

"Jo, I think we've got another piece of that code."

"Be right there."

Johnston's mood suddenly picked up, her heartache momentarily forgotten as her mind shifted to work. She quickly gathered her belongings, leaving behind her unfinished salad, and rushed out of the cafe.

Once back at work, Johnston wasted no time, and went straight to the analyst's desk. They greeted each other with a sense of urgency, both eager to get on with their business.

"So that next batch of numbers and letters was actually a set of..."

Johnston waved him on. "Just get to the part where you tell me what it means."

"White Horse Lounge."

Johnston squinted her eyes as she tried to figure out what it meant. "It's a business?"

The analyst bobbed his head. "I've already done a precursory check on it, and there are several White Horse Lounges all over the world."

"Still, there can't be too many places named that. How many more words are left to decipher?"

"I think there's two."

"Any ideas yet?"

He shook his head. "Not even a guess."

"All right, stay on it. Thanks."

"You got it."

Johnston went back to her desk and sat down, staring at her computer screen. She wasn't doing anything on it yet. She was just staring, tapping her fingers on the desk, thinking of all the information she had available. She then grabbed her phone and dialed Holt's number. He picked up right away.

"Hey, you got a second?"

"Sure," Holt replied.

"We got another piece of that code. It's White Horse Lounge. Does that mean anything to you now?"

"White Horse Lounge. I don't think so. Never been in one. Don't think I've ever even heard of it before."

"I was hoping maybe you'd been in one on a past assignment, something that didn't make it in a report."

"Afraid not."

Johnston put her hand on her head, not sure how he was going to respond to what she was about to say. But she had to put it out there.

"Listen, I, uh, think it's time to bring other people into this. We've got this place, we've got The Black Phoenix, maybe Pelligrini ties in... I'm not sure how much longer I can keep this quiet. If I start digging into this stuff, people are going to notice. And they're gonna start asking questions. I don't know how long I can hold off."

"OK."

Johnston seemed startled. She wasn't expecting

that reply. She was bracing herself for an argument. Or at least something more than a one word response.

"Did you hear me?"

"Yeah," Holt answered.

"I said I would like to bring other people in."

"I heard you. It's probably a good idea."

She scrunched her eyebrows together. She wasn't sure if she was still talking to the same man.

"You're OK with it?"

"Like you said, The Black Phoenix raises the stakes a little more. It's not some random hitman they found off the internet. This is a premier group. And if we're gonna find them, we're gonna need help."

Johnston breathed a sigh of relief. "I thought you were gonna fight me on that."

Holt chuckled. "I may be difficult sometimes, but I'm not unreasonable. But I want this understood, whoever you bring in, whoever you tell about this, whatever happens, it doesn't necessarily mean that I'm back in the fold. If they decide to work on this with me, it's not a favor that I need to repay. I want that to be crystal clear."

"It is. No strings attached. I'll, uh, I'll present it to Barnes."

"OK. Let me know how he takes it."

They hung up, and Johnston sighed, nervous about presenting this to Barnes. She knew he wouldn't be eager about doing this without a clear commitment from Holt about coming back. She also wasn't sure how she was going to do this without making it obvious that she'd been working with Holt on the side for the past few days without his knowledge. She gathered the various information from her desk, ready to march into Barnes' office.

"Well, here goes nothing."

15

Johnston took a deep breath and knocked on Barnes' office door. She heard his muffled voice calling for her to come in, and she pushed the door open. Barnes looked up from his desk, his expression serious and focused.

"Sir, I have something I need to talk to you about."

Barnes motioned for her to sit down. "What is it, Johnston?"

She sat down, not quite sure how to begin. "It's... about Holt."

Barnes suddenly looked more upbeat, hoping for good news. "Oh? Have you reeled him in?"

"Uh, well, not quite. I mean, not yet. But... I'm hopeful."

"So what about him?"

"Well..." Johnston moved her hands around, as if she were trying to find the right words. She wasn't finding them. It was a rather uncomfortable silence for a bit.

"What are you trying to say?"

Johnston sighed, knowing she just had to come out with it. "Holt is halfway around the world right now, trying to look for the people responsible for murdering his wife."

"I already know that."

Johnston raised an eyebrow. "You do?"

"Did you really think I'm not keeping up with him? He's important to this agency. I want him back in the fold. I sent people to keep an eye on him at his house and they reported back that he wasn't there. A little digging turned up he took a trip to Germany. How am I doing so far?"

"Oh, good. Yeah, very good. He's taken a few additional trips since then."

"The question I have is why I'm just hearing about this from you now?"

"Yeah, well, as you may be aware, he has some trust issues that he's sorting through."

Barnes smiled and chuckled. "Trust issues. Yeah."

"So, with that in mind, he has asked me to keep what he'd been doing private. So in order to gain his trust, I thought it'd be best to do as he asked."

Barnes clasped his hands together, his elbows on his desk, holding his hands just in front of his chin.

"Jo, is he working for us or not?"

"Uh, well, you know, that is still an evolving thing."

The Nobody Man

"You're stalling."

"As of the moment, he is not. But I am hopeful that with some time, and us helping him with this, that he will eventually be willing to return."

"Why exactly are you here?"

"Oh, well, we've uncovered a few things, and I was hoping to get a little more help and resources to put on it."

"So let me get this straight," Barnes said. "He is not currently working for us. It sounds like you've been helping him without telling anyone. You want us to devote additional time and resources into something that really doesn't involve us. You want to help a man who doesn't work for us commit an illegal act, and a personal vendetta. And you don't know where this is going to lead. Do I have that about right?"

Johnston uncomfortably smiled. "Um, well... yeah. That sounds about... right."

"I hope you know what you're doing with this."

As she usually did, she was able to finally put her nervousness aside and started talking with more conviction. She often had the habit of being anxious, especially when around superiors, or other people she really respected. But that nervous energy usually subsided at some point, especially when there was something she was talking about that she really believed in. This was one of those times.

She sat up a little straighter. "Sir, you asked me to do what I could to bring him in. I assume you knew that would be a difficult task. You obviously have known him a lot longer than I have. We've tried to bring him in before and nothing's worked. Right now, he needs this. He's lost, he's hurt, he's in pain, and his head is spinning. He wants justice, and he wants revenge. And he needs closure."

"And you think we can give that to him?"

Johnston nodded. "I do. I have offered him my help in whatever way I can give him with no questions asked, and no promises of him coming back. Just my help."

"That's a risky strategy."

"It's not much of a risk when nothing else has worked. He needs to trust me. He needs to know that I won't betray him, and that I'll do exactly what I say I will. And he won't do anything until he settles this. And once he does, I'm hopeful that he'll see that he still has a future here."

"And if he doesn't?"

"Then I've given it my best shot."

Barnes leaned back in his chair as he studied her. "All right. Run with it. Do what you think is best. But I can't have an ex-operative running all around the world on a personal revenge tour killing everything in sight. If there's any blowback, I need to know about it so I can make any denials, if need be."

"Understood, sir."

"I also want to be brought up to date every day

The Nobody Man

about what's going on." He then pointed at her. "And I want to hear it from you."

"I will."

"Before you leave every day, or if something major breaks out, I expect to be briefed on it."

"Absolutely."

"What do you have so far?" Barnes asked.

Johnston had a folder in her hand that she placed on his desk. "So far, Holt has visited Detlef Altmann, Gabriel Boucher, and Giorgio Pelligrini."

Barnes' eyes never left the information packet in front of him. "Pelligrini and Boucher, he worked with. Altmann was a job."

"Yes, I know. He's already cleared Boucher and Altmann. He doesn't feel they're involved."

"And Pelligrini?"

"He's dead."

Barnes finally looked back up upon hearing the news.

Johnston put her hands up, anticipating his next question. "Holt didn't do it. He found Pelligrini in the basement of his home in Sicily. He'd been tortured before being killed. But Holt searched the house and found some type of code. It's on the next page there."

Barnes flipped the page to look at it.

"As you can see, we've identified part of it. White Horse Lounge. Now whether this code is related to Holt's case, that we still don't know. It could be. It is a coincidence Holt's wife is killed, then a man who knows Holt's name is murdered in the same time period. And beaten, to boot, as if they were trying to get information out of him."

"Like The Nobody Man's name, perhaps?"

"Yeah. There's more." Johnston motioned for her boss to flip to the next page. "Holt got a picture of this man leaving his property on one of his security cameras the night his wife was killed."

Barnes looked at the picture. "Identify him?"

"Not yet, no. But, I do believe I've identified the logo on his hat."

The director's eyes looked further down at some of Johnston's scribblings. The name jumped out at him.

"The Black Phoenix?"

"I've pieced together what we see in that photo and compared it to the known logos in our database. It looks like a match."

"Do you know who they are?"

"Holt has already filled me in."

"They've been a ghost organization for over twenty years. We've never been able to pin any of them down. Or even get a name associated with anybody."

"Well, if this is right, they're the ones that killed Holt's wife."

Barnes leaned back a little, putting his hand over his face as he processed this information. This was a major development.

"Do we think White Horse Lounge has something to do with The Black Phoenix?"

"I don't know yet," Johnston answered. "I certainly think it's possible. That's partially why I need additional resources. I know how big this is and I could use all the help I can get."

"You've got it. Whatever you want, whoever you need, pull them in."

"I want to do a deep dive on Pelligrini, especially over the past month or two. I have a feeling he's the key in all this. If he was tortured over knowing Holt, and this White Horse Lounge code also refers to Holt, then figuring out where he's been and who he's talked to in the last weeks of his life will be vital."

"And what if you're wrong? What if it has nothing to do with Holt? Maybe he was working on something else that got him killed."

Johnston gulped. "Well, in that case, then we can move on to other things. And we still have The Black Phoenix. We know they're involved in this somehow. We just have to figure out how. But what I'm hoping is that we can tie Pelligrini to The Black Phoenix. And this White Horse Lounge. And if we can do that…"

Barnes finished her sentence, grinning at the prospect of finally hitting The Black Phoenix organization. "If we can do that… then we unleash the beast."

16

While Johnston and the rest of her team continued trying to work on the rest of the code, and all the other things they were working on, Holt wasn't going to just sit around and wait for them. That wasn't his style. He liked to be proactive. Especially on this. This was about his wife's murder. Nobody was more invested in getting to the bottom of it than he was.

Holt had already packed his bags, ready to embark on a journey that would take him deep into the heart of the criminal underworld. He couldn't rely solely on the agency to crack this case. To truly uncover the truth, he would have to step outside those boundaries and venture into the shadows where The Black Phoenix lurked. Wherever it may be.

As he got off the plane in Sicily, Holt's mind raced with a mix of determination and anger. Sicily was where it all began, where Pelligrini had been tortured and killed. Holt knew that delving into Pelligrini's recent activities would be a crucial starting point in unraveling the mystery.

There was someone who knew Pelligrini well. Someone he trusted. It was a name that never made it into the CIA's files. Or anyone else's, for that matter. Pellegrini hid the fact that this man sometimes worked with him. He operated in the background. But Holt knew. Pelligrini trusted Holt enough to even meet the man on a few occasions.

Angelo Calabrese owned a boat in Palermo. He rented it out for tourists, where he'd take them sailing, or snorkeling, or just dropping anchor in the middle of the sea if that's what they preferred. Holt had a hunch that Angelo Calabrese might hold the key to unlocking some crucial information about Pelligrini's activities before his death.

Holt made his way to the picturesque harbor in Palermo. The sound of seagulls filled the air as he scanned the area for Angelo's boat. Finally, he spotted it, a sleek vessel with the name "Re Marinaio" elegantly emblazoned on its side. Sailor King.

Holt approached the boat with a mixture of anticipation and caution. It'd been a long time since he last saw Calabrese. As he stepped onto the deck, a tall, weathered man with salt-and-pepper hair emerged from the cabin. Calabrese's blue eyes studied Holt for a moment before a small smile tugged at the corners of his lips.

"Good day, Signore Holt," Calabrese greeted him in a thick Sicilian accent. "What brings you here today?"

Holt extended his hand, returning the smile. "Angelo, it's been too long."

"Indeed it has. Three, four years, maybe?"

"Something like that."

Calabrese stuck his arm out towards a seat. "Sit, sit. What brings you out here? On vacation?"

Holt grinned. "I wish I was."

Calabrese studied Holt's face. There was a man with the weight of the world on it.

"Judging by your face, you are here for... a more ominous reason."

Holt nodded, looking up at the bright blue sky. "Did you know that Giorgio is dead?"

Calabrese looked at him in an unbelieving manner. Judging by his expression, Holt figured he was breaking news to him.

"Giorgio is dead?" Calabrese stammered. "Uh, uh... that cannot be. I just saw him two weeks ago. He was fine. Perfect health. Are you sure?"

"Yeah, I'm sure," Holt solemnly replied.

"You're positive it's Giorgio?"

"I saw him with my own two eyes. He was beaten and killed. Tied up in a chair in his basement."

Calabrese was stunned. He shifted in his seat, running his hands over his hair and his face, stopping them and leaving them over his mouth as he processed the news.

"I don't believe it."

"Wasn't a pretty sight."

"Why? Who would do this?"

Holt shook his head. "I don't know. That's partially why I'm here."

"Partially?"

"If you recall, I left the business a few years ago."

"I remember. You, me, and Giorgio drank a toast to your good health. And your wife, if I recall. I remember that was the main reason for your leaving. She was not well."

"Yeah. Someone killed her a week ago."

Calabrese instantly put his hand over his heart, saddened by the news. He then put his hand on Holt's knee in solidarity.

"I am truly sorry, my friend."

"What was Giorgio working on?"

"Nothing." Calabrese noticed the distrustful eye that Holt gave him. He put his right hand up as if to swear. "No, really. Giorgio did one more job, a few months after our last outing. He did not enjoy it. Said he was ready to give it up. He wanted nothing else to do with the life. And ever since then, we've both lived quiet lives until now. He immersed himself in his wine collection. And I immersed myself in my boat."

Holt leaned back and looked out at the sea. "I think their murders are connected somehow."

Calabrese looked bewildered. "What would one have to do with the other?"

Holt shrugged. "Just a hunch."

"No, no. You do not operate on hunches alone. Not without at least some basis of evidence to lead you there."

"What do you know about White Horse Lounge?"

Calabrese sat in silence for several seconds as he thought about it. "Nothing. What is that?"

"Not sure yet, myself."

"What about The Black Phoenix?" Holt asked.

Calabrese raised an eyebrow. Now that was a name he'd heard before. His face indicated the seriousness that the name bestowed. He looked around, almost as if someone was watching or listening. That's how revered The Black Phoenix was. Nobody wanted to hear the name in their presence.

"The Black Phoenix? How are they involved?"

Holt took out the picture of the man in the red hat and handed it over. Calabrese paid close attention to it.

"I believe that's the man that killed my wife. Taken on my property the night she was murdered. The CIA has matched the logo on his hat to The Black Phoenix."

Calabrese took a gulp, his eyes almost bulging out. "Why would they be after you? Or, your wife?"

"All I can figure is someone from my past, someone I hurt, wanted revenge on me by killing her."

Calabrese bobbed his head, understanding the

logic behind it. "What would this have to do with Giorgio?"

"Best as we can figure is that whoever set this up, didn't know my real name. It took them some time to find it."

Calabrese knew what he was getting at. "And you think that Giorgio provided it?"

Holt lifted his hands. "It's a theory. He was bound, tied, and beaten. Even if he did give it, I don't hold any ill will towards him. There's a reason torture's effective. Everybody succumbs to it at some point. It's just a matter of how long you can hold out."

Calabrese leaned back and folded his arms. "It's unbelievable."

"I searched through Giorgio's study. Found a piece of paper on his desk. Some type of code. I couldn't make it out. Sent it to some CIA contacts, and they've only decoded half the message. White Horse Lounge. Any ideas?"

"Ah, so that's from Giorgio?" Calabrese shook his head. "White Horse Lounge. It is still not familiar."

"He wasn't working on anything else?"

"Not to my knowledge."

"Then why the code?"

"That I cannot say."

"When's the last time you saw him?" Holt asked.

"It was about two weeks ago." Calabrese's eyes widened as he thought about it. "We actually met by accident. It was a small cafe. We've both met there for lunch or dinner many times before."

"But not this time?"

"No. This was pure chance. I was actually taking a picture, and I just happened to notice him sitting there with another man."

"Someone you recognized?"

Calabrese shook his head. "No. But Giorgio's mannerisms seemed off as he talked to this man. The other man did most of the talking. But Giorgio seemed withdrawn."

"Did he see you?"

"Not at first. I went to the other end of the cafe, where I could still see them, but I wasn't in their line of sight."

"How long did this conversation go on for?"

"Maybe ten minutes?"

"After the man left, I walked up to Giorgio's table. He was still sitting there. I pretended as if I just happened to come along at that moment. He looked distraught. I wouldn't say terrified, but he looked deeply concerned about something."

"Did you ask what?"

"I asked if he was OK, he smiled, and said it was nothing. I left it at that. I figured if he wanted me to know, he would've told me."

"Can you describe this man?"

Calabrese's face brightened, and he touched his

The Nobody Man

nose, before pointing at Holt. "I can do you even better. I took a picture of him."

Holt's mood suddenly improved. "You got a photo?"

Calabrese smiled as he got up. "Yes! Yes! I don't know why, but maybe because of the tone of their conversation, it didn't feel right to me. I thought I would take it in case Giorgio needed help with it at some point. We haven't seen each other since that night, so I had forgotten about it. Let me get my phone."

Calabrese got up, then went down below into the cabin to grab his phone. He emerged topside again a minute later. He scrolled through his pictures, of which there were many. He loved taking nature pictures. Finally, he stopped as he found the one he was looking for. He showed it to Holt.

"Can I copy this?"

"Sure! By all means."

Holt took a picture of it with his phone. He compared it with the one with the man in the red hat. They weren't the same guy. If they were, that would have made it an obvious connection. But Holt still believed they were connected somehow. The picture Calabrese took was a clear shot of the man's face. He was probably in his thirties, well dressed, short hair. Holt had never seen him before, but maybe this guy was associated with the White Horse Lounge in some way. Maybe Pelligrini was looking into them, whoever they were.

"How does all this connect together?" Calabrese asked.

"I wish I knew."

They sat there for the next few minutes, mostly in silence. Eventually, Holt figured he wasn't getting any more information, and it was time to exit. He shook hands with Calabrese.

"I appreciate all your help."

"You are welcome. If The Black Phoenix is involved in this, you must be cautious."

"I will be," Holt replied.

"Be careful. You know what they are capable of."

"The same could be said to them. They also know what I'm capable of. And I aim to deliver."

17

Holt stepped off the boat, eager to let Johnston know about the man sitting with Pelligrini. He pulled out his phone and called her number.

"Hey, I was just thinking about you."

"Having nightmares, are you?"

Johnston laughed. "Stop. I'm serious."

"So was I."

"Really?"

"Anyway, I was calling because I just talked to a former associate of Pelligrini's."

Johnston instantly started shuffling papers around on her desk. "I don't recall seeing anything about an associate."

"You don't really think everything that goes on out here makes it into those reports, do you?"

"Uh, no, no, I guess not."

"In any case, this guy told me that he saw Pelligrini

sitting with this man, in a not-so-friendly conversation, and he actually took a picture of the guy."

"Oh, that's great," Johnston said. "Can you send it over?"

"Yeah, I'll..."

Holt's thought process was interrupted as he started looking around. There were a number of people around, most of them looking like they worked there, or were tourists. But there was someone sitting down on the ground, directly ahead of him, that had a different kind of feel. He wasn't dressed like a tourist. And he didn't look like someone who worked a boat.

The man had sunglasses on, an oversized button-down shirt that wasn't buttoned, jeans, and brown work boots. Holt knew the type. The man had his head leaning back against the concrete wall, just kind of staring up at the sky, trying to remain inconspicuous.

"Aaron?"

Holt didn't reply. He then turned his head to his right. He saw a similar-looking man standing there. Not too close. But he just kind of seemed to be standing around doing nothing. Holt calmly turned his head in the other direction, and saw a third man to his left. He was just leaning up against a wooden table that was near the water.

"Aaron, you all right?"

Like a computer, his mind was racing with different possibilities. Who were these men? What did

The Nobody Man

they want? How was he going to escape? Where would he go? And finally, how would he kill them?

"I'm gonna have to call you back."

"Aaron, what's going on? What's happening?"

"Looks like I've got company."

"What? Where? I'll get you some help."

"Not enough time. I'll send you that picture. I'll take care of the rest."

"Aaron, let me do something."

"You can. Analyze the photo I'm about to send you. Hopefully you'll have something for me the next time I call."

"Please let me know when... that you're OK."

"Worrying about me already?"

"Please, just be careful."

"Will do."

Holt hung up, then quickly sent her a message with the picture. He then put the phone in his pocket. He took a deep breath as he looked at the man in front of him. He turned his head one more time to look at the man to his right. Neither of them were making a move toward him yet. But there were a lot of people around. They probably wanted a quieter spot to try to take him out.

And Holt assumed they were there for no other reason. If it was just to talk or make contact, they would've done it. At least one of them would. They were staying back for the moment because they wanted to follow him. And there was only one reason they'd want to do that.

He scanned his surroundings, looking for a way out without drawing attention to himself. Holt turned and started walking briskly away from the waterfront, weaving through the crowd as inconspicuously as he could. The man sitting on the ground began to slowly rise, his eyes fixed on Holt. The two men who were flanking him moved in closer, clearly onto his attempt to escape. Or what they thought was his attempt to escape. Holt wasn't intending on getting away. He just wanted to lure them into a more advantageous position for him to do what he did best.

As Holt picked up his feet and started walking faster, the steps of the men following him did as well. Holt turned his head around to confirm they were still coming. As he neared the exit, Holt spotted a narrow alley leading away from the main thoroughfare. Making a split-second decision, he veered into the alley, his senses on high alert.

Holt moved swiftly through the narrow passageway. He looked at his surroundings for any potential escape routes or hiding spots. The alley opened up into a small courtyard with several doors lining the walls. The men were gaining ground on him.

Suddenly, Holt darted through the alley and made a run for it. The three men instantly took off after him. Holt quickly looked for a spot he could hide. It was a residential area, with doors lined up along the entire way. There were balconies overhead. Small cars and motorcycles littered the sides of the street.

About midway through the narrow street, there was an opening, a small intersection as the alley split into another street. Holt instinctively took the path to the left. Almost instantly, he saw a small flatbed truck to his right. There were various items in it. But it'd be good enough to hide.

Holt hopped right into the back, covering himself with a small white sheet that was there. He took out his gun and waited. He left just enough of an opening where he could still see the street he just came from. Seconds later, the three men appeared. They stopped and started looking around.

"He couldn't have gotten far," one of them said. "Let's split up. I'll go straight. You guys take the sides. Find him."

The men split up as planned, with one heading straight and the other two taking the side streets. Holt remained hidden in the back of the truck, waiting for the right time to strike. He didn't want to use his gun right away. The sound of the shot would instantly draw the attention of everyone in the area, bringing the other two right back to him. He had to wait for the perfect opportunity.

Holt stayed perfectly still as he watched the man who had gone straight walk past the truck, unknowingly just a few feet away from him. Holt looked down in the bed of the truck, seeing some loose twine. There was a little bit more than he would have liked, but he picked it up and started wrapping it around his fingers on both hands.

Holt waited a couple of seconds, as the man was moving slowly, taking his time to make sure he didn't miss something. With the man's back to him, Holt threw the sheet off of himself, and slowly stood up in the bed of the truck, making sure he didn't make any noises to give himself away.

He then leapt onto the man's back, perfectly positioning himself, and wrapping the twine around the man's neck in one smooth motion. Holt leaned back hard, the man instantly dropping his weapon under the weight and surprise of the attack. Holt continued pulling with all his might. Eventually, the two collapsed to the ground, with Holt's back taking the brunt of the fall. But he wasn't letting go.

The man scratched and clawed at the thread around his neck, desperately gasping for air. Realizing he couldn't get his fingers underneath the twine to give his skin some space, the man started flailing away, hoping he could do something, anything, to get Holt to release him. Holt moved his head to each side so the man couldn't put his fingers in his eye sockets, or his nose. That was the most obvious move the man could make.

Holt knew all the countermeasures, though. And he positioned himself to avoid them. Slowly, Holt could feel the energy starting to leave the man's body.

His defensive tactics began to lessen, and he didn't have the same gusto in fighting him off anymore. Finally, the man gave up the fight completely. He was gone.

Holt kept the pressure up for a few more seconds, just to make sure the man wasn't playing any tricks. He'd seen that game before. Then he let go once he knew the man was really gone. Holt forcefully pushed the man's body off him, and got back to his feet.

He knew he didn't have time to stay and comb through the man's pockets or anything, but he wanted to know who this guy was. He took out his phone and took a picture. That should give them some answers.

As soon as he was about to put his phone away, a shot rang out. Holt was startled and ducked, though the bullet had already gone past him. He looked to his left, observing one of the other men running towards him. He was still in the other alleyway.

Holt immediately took off running in the opposite direction. The other man gave chase. After a few minutes of running through several alleys, Holt eventually came to a large building that was probably an apartment building in a past life. Right now, a door was slightly hanging off, and there were cutouts for the windows, though there was no actual glass in them at the moment. It had all the signs of an abandoned building.

Holt went inside, looking around, seeing that it was no longer in use. Whether it was currently under construction, or there was just the remnants of its previous usage, there was trash and debris all over the place.

Holt knew he couldn't stay in the abandoned building for long. It would just be a matter of time before the other man caught up to him. He quickly scanned the area, looking for a way to create a distraction and gain some time. And also an advantage. Spotting a pile of wooden planks in the corner, Holt got an idea.

Grabbing a few of the planks, Holt arranged them near the entrance in such a way that it would make a loud noise if someone stepped on them. He then found some steps and went up to the second floor. The most obvious spot for him would be somewhere on the first floor. That's what the man behind him would be expecting. Holt tried not to do the conventional thing. That's how people got killed. Doing what was expected.

He still had two more planks in hand and put them in the open doorway. He positioned himself behind a crumbling wall, out of sight, and waited. He'd be able to hear when the man arrived.

It didn't take long for the sound of footsteps to approach the entrance. The man cautiously entered the building, his gun held out in front of him. As soon as he stepped on the planks, they creaked loudly under his weight. Holt heard it. He readied himself, knowing it wouldn't be too long until the man reached him.

A few minutes went by. Holt knew the man was probably taking his time to clear the first floor. Though the man tried to disguise his movements by walking slowly, it wasn't really possible. There was too much debris everywhere, including the steps, to walk around unnoticed.

Though it was faint, Holt heard the man coming. Within a minute, the man was just outside the room where Holt was waiting. He patiently waited for the man to make his move.

Then, the man took a step inside. He stepped on the wood board, breaking it in half. Startled, the man looked down for a moment. That was all the time Holt needed. He jumped out from behind the crumbling wall, pointing his gun at the man. The man looked up, seeing Holt standing there, though it was too late to do anything. By the time the man raised his arm, the bullet from Holt's gun had already penetrated his chest.

The man was knocked over onto his back; the gun falling from his hand. Holt walked over to the dead man's body and took his phone out again, snapping a picture of the man's face.

Holt suddenly perked up when he heard another noise. It sounded like someone else was entering the building. He could hear the crackling sound of debris breaking under someone's heavy footsteps.

He could've just waited there, but Holt didn't want to be caught in the same position. The last remaining man knew where he was. Holt liked to catch his victims by surprise. It was easier that way.

Knowing he couldn't go back the way he came, Holt looked around. There was an opening for another door that led to a small balcony. Holt hurried over to it. Just as there were no windows or doors, there was no railing for the balcony either. Holt looked down, seeing cars parked beneath him. It was about a ten or twelve foot jump.

Holt wasted no time. He jumped right onto the roof of a small car, putting a dent into the top of it. He quickly rolled off, and started running again. He was running towards a fenced area. He looked back, just in time to see the last man jumping from the same spot.

The fence was too high to climb on his own. At least quickly. So Holt took a leap onto the hood of a car parked in front of it, making his way up to the roof. He then jumped on the top of the fence, easily climbing over the rest of it.

The other man was still in pursuit. Holt landed on a metal roof structure that provided shade to a handful of cars that were parked underneath it. Holt ran across it for a few moments before jumping down to the concrete below.

As the other man climbed over the fence, Holt took cover between a couple of cars, waiting for his adversary to arrive. Holt looked up as he heard the man's thunderous steps land on the metal overhead. Holt quickly took up position several cars away. He made sure he was squatting right next to a tire, so his legs couldn't be seen if the man looked under the cars for a sign of him.

Holt stayed put, knowing eventually the man would walk past several cars, and come right into his line of fire. He just had to stay patient. Several minutes went by. Holt heard a small noise, as if a shoe skidded against the concrete. It was very close.

Holt remained stationary, pointing his gun at the air in front of him. He first saw the outline of the gun. Then the rest of the man appeared. Holt took careful aim and fired. The man went down. Holt got up and walked over to him. This man was dead too.

Holt did the same as with the others and took his picture. It would've been nice if he was only wounded, and Holt got some answers out of him. But that usually only happened in the movies. You never fired your gun with the intention of wounding someone so you could question them. If you fired, you shot to kill. A wounded man was still a dangerous enemy. One that could still kill you.

Now, that wasn't an option. Holt looked around, making sure there were no other surprises in wait. He never wanted to assume there was nothing else. Letting your guard down was a quick way to wind up in the cemetery. He tried not to.

He looked down at the dead man again. He'd never

seen him before. But he'd send the pictures to Johnston. Hopefully she'd be able to give them some more answers. And maybe they could figure out who these men were working for.

One way or another, though, Holt felt like they were getting closer. He wasn't sure to what yet. But he hoped these three dead men held the key to finding out.

18

Holt checked his surroundings, knowing he had to keep moving. He made his way out of the area, going as far in the other direction as he could, though he tried to stay out of open areas. He stuck to the alleys between buildings as much as he could. He needed to find a safe space to lie low and regroup.

After moving for about half an hour, he found a secluded spot, behind a car in a corner of an alley, his back resting against the cold concrete wall. He took out his phone to call Johnston to clue her in. She immediately picked up. There was a rushed tone in her voice that indicated her level of concern.

"Thank God you called, I've been so worried. Are you OK?"

"It's all taken care of," Holt replied.

"What happened? Are you hurt?"

"I don't know. Three guys found me down by the marina. Followed me for a bit."

"Did you lose them?"

"In a way. They're dead."

"Oh. OK. Um… anything I need to…?"

"There's nothing you have to clean up," Holt said.

"Are you injured or anything?"

"I'm good. Just figuring out my next step."

"Did you recognize any of them?"

"No. I took their pictures, though. Hold on, I'll send them to you."

Holt took the phone away from his ear and sent her a message, including the faces of the dead men.

"OK, I got them," Johnston said. "I'll start running them. Any ideas about who they are?"

"No clue."

"I'll see what I can come up with. Where are you right now?"

Holt looked up. "Just in some alley."

"Where are you heading?"

"I don't know. I'll probably head back to my hotel."

"No, don't do that."

"Why not?"

"These men found you somehow. How do you know they don't have other people waiting at the hotel?"

"Good point."

"Do you have anything there you need to get?" Johnston asked.

"No, everything's in the car."

"Just get to your car and start driving. I'll book you a hotel somewhere. Then you just have to make sure you're not followed."

"Thanks."

"I'm here for you."

"Anything on that other picture I sent you?" Holt asked.

"Not yet. Still running it down. I'll add these new ones to the list. Maybe by the time you get to the hotel, I'll have something for you. Speaking of which, I should get to it. I'll send you a message with the address when I've booked something."

Holt ended the call and quickly got up from his spot. He made his way through the alleys, heading back to where his car was parked, near the marina. He made sure he kept clear of where the bodies were, though. He kept his head turning the entire way, making sure nobody else picked him up.

Thankfully, he saw no further signs of trouble. Once he had his car in sight, he stood near the end of the alley, just looking at it. He wanted to make sure there was nobody else just milling around, waiting for him to come back to it. Holt stood there for over ten minutes, just watching.

Satisfied that he was in the clear, Holt darted across the street until he reached his car. He quickly got in and started the engine. He pulled out onto the road, continuously checking his mirrors for signs that he was being followed. But there was no one. For fifteen minutes, he drove without the slightest of worries about being followed. There were no cars that seemed glued to him.

He received a text from Johnston, letting him know the address of the hotel she booked for him. He continued driving aimlessly for another twenty minutes, wanting to make sure that nobody else would find the hotel after him.

Finally, Holt arrived at the hotel Johnston had booked for him. It was a small, nondescript place on the outskirts of town. He parked his car in a secluded spot, in a remote corner of the parking lot, ensuring the vehicle was not easily visible from the main entrance. Holt grabbed his bag from the trunk and headed inside, keeping a watchful eye on his surroundings.

Once inside, the receptionist barely glanced up as he checked in, which suited Holt just fine. The less attention, the better. He took the key to his room and made his way up the creaky stairs to the second floor. Finding his room at the end of a dimly lit corridor, he entered and locked the door behind him.

As he entered the room, Holt tossed his bag on the floor. He had to do a sweep of the room, checking every nook and cranny for any signs of intrusion. After everything checked out, Holt's eyes went to the window. He walked over to it, checking the sightlines, making sure there were no vantage points where a potential sniper could be lying in wait. Satisfied with what he saw, he closed the curtains and sat down at the small table.

He took a deep breath, trying to calm his racing thoughts. The events of the day swirled around in his mind, each detail demanding attention. He put his hand on his head, thinking back to his final days with Denise. He closed his eyes, wishing she was still in front of him. He was conflicted. He felt he was making progress, and yet at the same time, he didn't feel like he was closer at all.

What Holt really needed was a new lead. He needed Johnston to come through for him and find something out on at least one of the four faces he'd recently given her. One of them had to lead somewhere. Right now, all he really knew was that The Black Phoenix was involved. Unfortunately, no one knew who or where they were. Right now, the ball was in her court.

~

Johnston was swiveling her chair around as she split her concentration between two computers. She had her desktop in front of her, and her laptop to the right. Another analyst scurried over to her desk, putting a piece of paper down on it when they arrived.

"We got a hit on your guy."

Johnston immediately looked down. "Which one? I'm waiting on four, you know."

"Oh. Um, the guy at the cafe."

"Oh, OK. That one. What do you got?"

"His name is Theo Florakis. Greek national. Owns a flower shop. No ties to any criminal organizations that I can tell."

Johnston picked up the paper with Florakis' picture front and center, reading the information on him.

"So what was he doing with a former associate of Holt's? Who just so happens to get killed not so long after talking to him."

The other analyst shrugged. "Guess that's your department."

Johnston sighed. "Yeah. How are we on those other three?"

"Database is still going through them. Good shots of their faces, so it shouldn't take long to identify them. Probably within the hour."

Johnston forced a smile. "Thanks."

As the analyst left, Johnston typed Florakis' name in, seeing if she could uncover any additional facts about him. What she'd been given was just the brief rundown. Now she had to dig deep. But as the minutes passed, there wasn't much more to be uncovered. Florakis seemed to be a normal, everyday type of guy. There was no folder on him. His name wasn't on any watch list. He was just a regular person. At least, according to the information at hand. But that was obviously not true.

There had to be a connection somewhere. It was no coincidence in Johnston's mind that Florakis met with a man who wound up dead a few days later. There was something going on.

After an hour of searching, and coming up empty, Johnston finally gave up on the matter. There was nothing else she was going to find. She was hoping to give Holt a lot of ammunition to work with. As it stood, she only had a name. She grabbed her phone and called Holt to give him the news.

"Hey, you got something for me?"

"A name," Johnston said. "The man that Pelligrini was sitting with at that cafe is Theo Florakis."

"Who's that?"

"That's the problem. He doesn't appear to be anybody. He owns a flower shop in Greece. We don't have a jacket on him. He's literally nobody."

"He's obviously somebody," Holt replied, bringing up the picture of Florakis on his phone. "We just don't know who yet."

"I just checked flight records before I called. He booked a plane trip from Greece to Sicily, and then a day later, from Sicily back to Greece."

"Sounds like maybe it was just to have that meeting with Giorgio."

"Yeah, maybe."

"Probably not involved in his death," Holt said. "I

think we're looking at a span of a couple days to a week between that meeting and when Giorgio was killed. Florakis would have been gone by then."

"So who is this guy?"

Holt continued staring at the photo. "I don't know. But I aim to find out."

19

Johnston put her hot morning coffee down on her desk and rubbed her face to get the sleep out of her eyes. With Holt traveling to Athens, Greece to meet with Theo Florakis, Johnston turned her attention to the other three men that Holt killed. She was convinced they would hold some answers once their identities were uncovered.

She stretched her arms out and sat down, noticing the strange file on her desk. It wasn't there when she left the previous night. She opened it, immediately seeing three information sheets. It had pictures, names, and brief highlights of the people described.

These were the people that Holt killed the day before. She quickly scanned through the information sheets, her eyes widening with each passing sentence. First up was Viktor Petrov, a former Russian military officer turned mercenary. Known for his ruthless tactics and lack of mercy, Petrov had been involved in several high-profile assassinations and acts of sabotage across Europe. He was a known player in the CIA's eyes.

Second was Zhang Wei, a former member of China's Ministry of State Security, or MSS, which was the CIA's equivalent. Like Petrov, he'd also been rumored to be involved in numerous high-profile assassinations across Europe and Asia.

Third on the list was Marcus Greene, a UK national. He was a Captain in the British Army. Special Forces. The sheet on him wasn't quite as long or extensive as the other two. He seemed to be relatively new on the scene of high-profile assassins.

Johnston could sense the pieces of the puzzle slowly falling into place, yet the bigger picture remained elusive. How any of them were connected to The Black Phoenix wasn't yet clear, if they even were at all. They all had ties to military or intelligence agencies and specialized in covert operations.

Even if the big picture couldn't be seen yet, one thing was clear. They were after Holt. The fact that all three had different backgrounds, and nationalities, indicated a specific person, or group, was behind it. Perhaps it was The Black Phoenix. Maybe they'd finally got a fix on a few of their members, even though they were now dead.

Though it would have been preferable if the men were still alive and could talk, dead men could still reveal quite a bit. Phone records, rental cars, hotels, plane trips, all were small pieces of a larger puzzle. All of the men would have been quite secretive with all that information, but now that they were dead, Johnston could work backwards. She knew where they wound up. Now she could figure out where they came from.

She took a sip of her coffee. This was going to be a long day.

∽

Holt stepped into the small flower shop. The bell above the door jingled softly as Holt walked in. He was immediately hit with the scent of fresh flowers. Holt took a quick scan of the shop. The walls were lined with colorful arrangements, and a few potted plants sat near the window, basking in the sunlight. Colorful bouquets adorned the space, casting a vibrant aura in the otherwise serene atmosphere.

Theo Florakis, a middle-aged man with a warm smile, looked up from arranging a bouquet of lilies at the counter. That smile faltered when he recognized the customer. His eyes held a mixture of curiosity and caution as he looked at Holt standing in the doorway. Holt noted the distinct lack of surprise on Florakis' face, indicating that he had been expecting this visit.

"Can I help you find something special today?" Florakis asked, with a slight, welcoming accent.

Holt stepped closer, keeping his voice low. "I'm not here for flowers, Mr. Florakis. We need to talk."

"What can I help you with?"

Holt got straight to the point. "I'm here to ask you a few questions about your recent visit to Sicily."

Florakis paused in his flower arrangement, his expression turning serious. "I'm afraid I don't know what you're talking about. I haven't been to Sicily in months."

Holt raised an eyebrow, unconvinced by the denial. "We have evidence that suggests otherwise. You met with a man named Giorgio Pelligrini." He then pulled out his phone and showed him the picture of the two of them at the cafe. "Would you like to issue another denial?"

A slight grin formed on Florakis' face. "No, Mr. Holt. I don't think that will be necessary."

Holt moved his head slightly, surprised that the man already knew his name.

"How do you know me?"

"Let's just say I have connections in high places, Mr. Holt. And your reputation precedes you." Florakis straightened up, his demeanor shifting slightly. "I am a businessman, Mr. Holt. I run a humble flower shop in Greece. As for my recent meeting with Giorgio, let's just say it was a matter of mutual interest."

"Whose?"

"Yours, of course."

Holt was starting to get an eerie feeling about this. His head started shifting, looking out of the corners of his eyes, almost expecting an ambush at any moment. Florakis noticed his awareness shifting.

"You are in no danger here, Mr. Holt."

"Then maybe it's about time you tell me what's going on here. Why were you two meeting about me?"

Florakis suddenly looked disturbed. He motioned for Holt to follow him to a back office, where they could sit and talk. It was a small room that barely fit a desk and chairs. But it suited the purpose.

"Why were you in Sicily?" Holt asked.

Florakis rubbed his face. "I was in Sicily to warn Giorgio about the impending threat."

"Meaning The Black Phoenix?"

Florakis looked away and stared at the wall, as if he were remembering something. "Yes, The Black Phoenix."

"Was Giorgio involved with them?"

"Not in the way you might think."

"Then explain it."

"I had gotten word that The Black Phoenix was going to target him. I went there to warn him."

"Why would you?"

"Because I've known Giorgio for a few years through various endeavors. I knew what The Black Phoenix would do to him once they found him."

"So they are the ones that killed him?"

Florakis nodded. "Yes."

"That brings up more questions."

"I can anticipate a few."

"Why'd they target him?" Holt asked.

"They were made aware of your connection to each other. They wanted him to tell them your real name."

"How'd they latch on to him?"

"That I do not know."

"How'd you find out about it to begin with?"

Florakis hesitated for a moment. "I have certain backdoor channels with The Black Phoenix."

"You know them?"

"I used to be with them."

Holt's eyes almost bulged out, not expecting that answer. His hand instinctively went down to his side, where his weapon was holstered. Florakis noticed his guest's movements.

"You will not need that."

"You're with The Black Phoenix?"

Florakis shook his head. "Not anymore."

"How's that possible? I heard once you're in, you're in for life."

"That is mostly true. In most cases, the only way you leave the organization is if you die, or you retire."

"I assume you did the latter?"

"Not quite. I simply had enough and walked away."

"I find it hard to believe they'd just allow that to happen."

Florakis simply lifted up his shirt, revealing a scar, near his heart, where he'd been shot.

"They did not. But I did make a truce with them."

"How's that work?" Holt asked.

"I protected myself. I have various documents in safe places all over the world. In the event of my untimely death, those documents would get released to several governments, all of whom would be quite interested in what they reveal. Instead, with the promise those documents never see the light of day, I get left alone. I get to live in peace."

"So you were an assassin?"

"No. I have a knack for acquiring information. Getting what's necessary behind the scenes. That was my role."

Holt finally took his hand off his weapon, feeling he wouldn't have to use it just now. He sighed.

"Someone hired them to kill my wife."

Florakis looked saddened. "Yes, that was my understanding."

"Do you know who? And why?"

"That information did not come to me."

"Do you still know who is in the organization?"

"Most. Do they frequently recruit?"

"Not frequently, no. They only invite those that are truly elite in their skills. And those who are elite in hiding in the shadows and keeping their mouths shut. Both skills are hard to find."

"If I showed you pictures, would you be able to identify them?"

"Before we get to that, are you sure you were not followed here?"

"I was not," Holt answered. He took out his phone and scrolled to the man in the red hat. "I think this is the guy that killed my wife."

Holt handed the phone over, and Florakis took a look. "Yes, he is a member. I'm surprised you got such a good picture of him. Where was it taken?"

"On my property the night she was killed. Hidden cameras."

"An intelligent precaution on your part."

"Most of these guys work together?"

"No. You could have ten of them standing in the same room, and none of them would know each other. They all usually work alone. They do not care about nationality, race, or religion. They are completely independent in all facets."

"Why kill my wife? Why not come after me?"

"They only do what they're hired to do."

"Who's behind it?"

"That I cannot say. I have no idea."

Holt pointed to his phone. "Scroll to the next three pictures."

Florakis did, seeing the faces of the men that Holt killed in Sicily. "Two of these are Black Phoenix members. The third one I have not seen before."

"Which two?"

"Viktor Petrov and Zhang Wei."

"The third one is a guy named Marcus Greene."

"Could be a newer member. They all look deceased."

"They are," Holt said. "I killed them. They were following me."

"Impressive work."

"I thought you said they don't typically work together."

"They usually don't. A man such as yourself is a special case, though. They assume one man will not be enough for you."

"But why try to take me out now? They came to my house and killed my wife. Why not wait for me to show up there? Doesn't make sense that they'll try to kill me now."

Florakis lifted his hands as if he wasn't sure. "Perhaps they weren't hired to kill you initially. Plans sometimes change. Or maybe they didn't believe you'd be here investigating. Maybe you're getting too close. Or maybe there is some other reason. Maybe they weren't trying to kill you."

Holt gave him a disbelieving eye. "Hard not to believe that."

"Perhaps there were three of them because they wanted to take you alive. Question you. Torture you. Take you prisoner. Not out of the question."

"How many people are involved in The Black Phoenix?"

"The last number I heard was over a year ago."

"And what was it?"

"17 agents. Several others behind the scenes, running the operation." Florakis looked at a picture of one of the dead men. "Well, less now."

Holt grabbed his phone and scrolled to the picture of the code he found at Pelligrini's house.

"What about this? You recognize it?"

Florakis briefly glanced at it and closed his eyes. "Yes."

"You know what it says?"

"It is a code that I taught to Giorgio. We invented it while with The Black Phoenix. Each letter is actually a different letter. And each number and shape corresponds to a different letter, as well. But it also depends on the shape, the style, what comes before or after. There are precautions built in to make it unreadable. Dummy letters. It is made to be complicated."

"So I hear. You know where I found that?"

Florakis shook his head. "No idea."

"In Giorgio's study."

"Trying to send you a message, no doubt."

"What does it say?" Holt asked.

Florakis licked his lips as he looked at the photo. "White Horse."

"I already know that part. White Horse Lounge. What's the rest? I'm gonna find out sooner or later. Might as well just speed the process up."

Florakis sighed. "If you go through with this, it is unlikely you will survive."

"I've already come to terms with that."

"If you back off, I could perhaps get word to them. You could still live if an agreement is made."

"That's not an option," Holt said. "They killed my wife. Everyone involved is going to pay."

"That could include you."

"Like I said, I'm OK with that. The rest of the message."

Florakis looked at the picture again. He still didn't want to say. But he knew Holt was not going to let it go. And he was not going to back down. He was going wherever this led.

"The information did not come from me."

"I forgot your name already," Holt replied.

"White Horse Lounge. Singapore. Zhi Kwon."

Holt's face was expressionless. It was just a blank stare. He wasn't sure what he expected the rest of the message to reveal, but it wasn't that. Maybe he just didn't expect to hear a name.

"Is this White Horse Lounge in Singapore?"

"Yes."

"What's so special about it?" Holt asked.

"It is often where Zhi Kwon does business."

"And who's Zhi Kwon?"

"He is one of the leaders. There is no one man that runs The Black Phoenix. There is a five-person council. They vote on matters."

"Everyone live in Singapore?"

"Agents are spread out across the world. To my knowledge, none of them live there."

"What about this council?" Holt wondered. "They all there?"

"Three of them were. I'm not sure about now."

"And the other two?"

"One lives in Hong Kong. The other lives in Tokyo. They get together at the White Horse to discuss business. Once every other week, I believe."

"I need the other names," Holt said. "Every person on the council. Every agent. Every address. Every place they do business. Everything."

"If I give this to you, you must finish the job in its entirety. If you do not, they will not ever stop looking for you. And you will not escape their grasp."

"Escaping wasn't exactly what I had in mind. I will kill every single person associated with The Black Phoenix. And then I'm going to kill the person that hired them. Nothing else is acceptable. It's all… or it's nothing."

20

Once Holt was done with Florakis, he went back to his hotel room. Considering he didn't have much in the way of luggage, there wasn't much to pack. He did call Johnston, however, to let her know what he found out.

"Hey, you know, I was thinking about these three dead guys, they had to follow you to that marina. I'd bet they had you tailed from the airport."

"Doesn't much matter now," Holt replied.

"Of course it does. If I'm gonna find out more info, I need to figure out where they've been."

"I already know who they are."

"What?"

"My conversation with Florakis was very productive."

"Oh?"

"The three dead guys are Black Phoenix agents."

"And he knows this how?"

"He used to work for them," Holt answered. "He heard my name, and that they were going to target Pelligrini to come after me. Florakis went there to warn him."

"Are you sure he's telling you the truth?"

"I felt he was being honest."

"OK. Well, that's, um..." she took a deep breath. "OK, so Pelligrini is the link. They beat him to find out your real name. So now..."

"There's more. Florakis decoded the rest of that message."

"Really?"

"Turns out he helped invent it. It's a Black Phoenix thing."

"What's it say?"

"White Horse Lounge. Singapore. Zhi Kwon."

"OOK? So, the White Horse Lounge is in Singapore. Who's Zhi Kwon?"

"One of the people that runs The Black Phoenix. Apparently there's a five-person council."

"OK, wow. This is... this is a lot of new information. I'll have to start running this down."

"I have the rest."

"What?"

"I have the names of the five people on the council. Three live in Singapore. One in Hong Kong. And one in Tokyo."

"So what does that mean for you?" Johnston asked.

"I'm gonna go there and kill each and every one of them."

"Aaron, there's still the matter of The Black Phoenix agents. We don't know how many there are."

"About fourteen now."

Johnston was almost dumbfounded. "And how do you know this?"

"Florakis gave me their names."

"And he just gave them to you?"

"We came to an understanding."

"What makes you think he's not setting you up?"

"Florakis left The Black Phoenix over five years ago. The only reason he's alive and remains alive is because he has information stored away that would get sent to the government to out them if he's killed. As long as he stays alive, that information never sees the light of day."

"And how do you figure into it?"

"Because he knows he's a loose end. He believes The Black Phoenix is actively searching for this information, and if they ever find it, he's as good as dead. He believes they eventually will find it, and then kill him, or they'll just kill him, and change their operation."

"Again, how does that involve you?"

"Because if I kill their leadership, none of that matters anymore," Holt said.

"So he's giving you this information, hoping you take care of The Black Phoenix for him?"

"I guess that's what it comes down to."

"Why hasn't he just done it himself? He could've hired others."

"I don't know. And to be honest, I don't care. All I care about... is that I've got the info I need right now. And I am going to do something about it."

"Which is what?"

"I'm gonna fly into Singapore, visit the White Horse Lounge, and take out everyone I come into contact with."

"No. That is the wrong idea."

"Josie, I don't need—"

"No, listen to me. You can't just fly into Singapore and go all John Wick on everybody. That's not going to work. If you wanna do this, and actually do it right, and be successful, and maybe even walk out of it at the end, you need a plan."

Holt was silent for a moment. "What do you suggest?"

"Right now, you're on their watch list. They know where you live, they know where you've been, and maybe they know where you're going."

"I'm not stopping."

"No one said you had to. But just think about it. They probably have someone watching the airports, so if you just fly in there, they're either gonna know you're on the flight list, or they're gonna spot you when you step off the plane. And they'll be long gone before you ever get to the White Horse Lounge. Assuming you're not killed in the airport bathroom."

Holt sighed, knowing she was probably right. But he also didn't want to delay either.

"Give me some time to come up with something."

"There is no time," Holt said. "I'll figure out a way to slip in there undetected."

Johnston feverishly started typing away, hoping to come up with something quickly. She could tell Holt wasn't going to sit around and wait for days and days. She had to come up with something that would appeal to him, and make herself feel at ease. And she had to do it fast.

"Malaysia."

"Huh?"

"You can fly into Malaysia," Johnston said. "Then drive into Singapore from there. We'll have to get you a new identity and paperwork, though."

"Why?"

"There are checkpoints to get into Singapore on the ground. How do you know they don't have contacts in the government there protecting them? We don't know how far their reach goes. You go in there flashing your real name, they get an alert, then they're gone. And we'd have lost our best chance at finding them."

"I could just find a boat and get in that way."

"You could. And you might have to fight your way in or out. Or you can do it my way, the easier way, and nobody will know you're there."

Holt sighed. He knew she was making sense. But right now, he didn't want sense. He just wanted revenge. He wanted to be there as soon as he could make it. No delays.

"Aaron, listen to me. I know how badly you want this. But let's be smart about it. I want you to get the justice you want, and the closure you need. I also want you to live through it. I'd like to talk to you again after this is over. And I mean hearing your voice. Not talking to you looking down at your grave."

"I didn't realize you'd come visit me."

"Of course I would. But let's not do it so soon, huh? Just give me some time?"

Holt was considering her pleas. "How much?"

"Just give me a day."

"Then it's gonna take additional time to get it to me."

"An additional day, tops. We're only talking about two days. It gives you, and us, time to devise a strategy so you don't just go in there blasting away and getting yourself killed. Especially if there's only three of them there. You still have to worry about the additional two. And you can't get to them if you don't do this right."

"Fine. I'll give you the time you need. But if I'm still sitting here on day three with my thumb up my ass, we're gonna do it my way."

"I promise it won't get to that."

"There's one other thing," Holt said. "Florakis gave me the names he remembered of the fourteen remaining agents. There could be more if they've hired additional people in the last year he doesn't know about."

"Really? You have all the names?"

"All the names he knew. I'll send them over."

"That's great! We can really dismantle their network."

"I'll send you the list. I would suggest a coordinated attack as much as possible. If it gets out they're being eliminated, whoever's left will go underground so far you'll never find them again. And I don't want it getting back to Singapore before I get there."

"Don't worry. To coordinate something against that many agents, it would take more than a few days' worth of planning, anyway."

"As soon as we hang up, I'll send it to you."

"Thanks. And Aaron?"

"Yeah?"

"Thank you for trusting me with this. I won't let you down."

He didn't know why, but he believed her. Trusted her. He hoped it wasn't misplaced.

"Just let me know when it's done, Josie."

Johnston smiled. "You're really gonna stick with that, aren't you?"

"Like I said, I think it suits you. Unless you're really against it."

"No, no. I can get used to it. As long as it doesn't catch on with anybody else."

"Sounds like a deal. Oh, hey, how's the thing with the boyfriend working out?"

Johnston hesitated for a second. "It's not. I broke up with him. I just can't move out there with him."

"You doing OK?"

She was a little flustered. It almost sounded like he was truly concerned about her. Maybe he was just going through the motions. But he sounded like he genuinely cared.

"Uh, yeah, yeah. You know, just keeping myself busy with work. Mostly with you. You're basically taking up all my time these days. I mean, how's a girl supposed to have a social life with someone like you hanging around?"

Holt laughed. "You can always cut me loose at any time."

"Not a chance. I think we might be stuck together. Hopefully, for a while. Even after this is over."

Holt had a delayed response. "Yeah. Maybe."

"Anyway, I'll get started on everything right away. I'll keep you updated every few hours so you know our progress."

"I appreciate that."

"Always. You can always count on me."

"Yeah. I'm beginning to see that."

21

Johnston knocked on the door to Barnes' office, which was already open. He was sitting behind his desk on the phone, but waved at her to come in. With some folders in hand, she sat down across from him, patiently waiting until he was finished. Once he hung up the phone, he took a sip of water.

"What's up?"

She put the folders down in front of him. "We've had a major breakthrough."

Barnes flipped open the folder and started reading. "What is all this?"

"The nucleus of The Black Phoenix organization."

Hardly believing it, Barnes more intently looked at the information. "How many names are here?"

"Nineteen. Fourteen are agents, and five are the head."

Barnes started rubbing his forehead, though he

didn't take his eyes off the folder. "How did we get all this?"

"Holt. While investigating what happened with Pelligrini, he came across someone else who knew him, who also apparently used to work with The Black Phoenix."

"And how do we know this person isn't feeding him bad intel?"

"I've spent the last few hours verifying it the best I could."

"And?"

"I believe it is correct. All fourteen of those men are former military or special agents for various governments. They all have very peculiar patterns in their movements over the past few years."

"Such as?"

"Phone records, passports, things that can be traced, everything is normal for a period of time. Then they go off grid for a few weeks. Passport will be stamped, then not another trace of them for a week or two. Nothing on their phone, credit cards, nothing. It's like they vanish. Then, they mysteriously pop up again when their passport gets a hit again."

"That doesn't exactly tie them to anything," Barnes said. "It just proves it's worth digging into further."

"Sir, I believe these are the people The Black Phoenix uses. If Holt does what I think he's about to, once these people get wind of it, they may all go into a hole. And we won't find them again."

"So what are you suggesting?"

"That we take them out now."

"And what if we're wrong about the intel? What if they're not working for them?"

Johnston was silent for a moment. She feared being wrong. She believed what she was saying. She believed Holt. But did she believe it one hundred percent, with complete conviction? These were peoples' lives at stake.

Barnes could see the sliver of doubt in her mind. "Here's what we'll do. We'll get agents in place. We'll find them. We'll put them under surveillance. No one will make a move until we know for sure. And that's what you will do. Find the connections. Take however many analysts you need to take in there and get them working on this. Find where all these agents were when any assassinations went down. Cross reference and check everything. Prove these people were there and responsible beyond any shadow of a doubt. Once you have that, then we'll give the order."

"These guys are professionals. What if they spot the surveillance?"

"If they make a run for it, the order changes immediately. Anyone who spots us and runs, assume they're guilty and take them out."

"Understood."

"Right now, this is a top priority. I want everyone on this."

"I'll pull whoever I have to," Johnston said.

"What's Holt's next move?"

"He's headed to Singapore."

"Why?"

Johnston pointed at the folder. "It's on the next page there."

Barnes flipped the sheet. "Zhi Kwon. One of the leaders. Him and two others are based there."

"That's right."

Barnes continued reading. "Kwon and Singapore are the rest of that code?"

"Correct."

"You've done an excellent job with this report."

Johnston smiled, though she wouldn't take much of the credit. "Thank you. Holt did most of the work, though. He's the one that got all the information. I just compiled everything together."

"But he gave it all to you. That's important. He's trusting you. You're building a rapport."

"I'm just trying to do right by him. Give him whatever he needs. Not lie to him."

"Keep it up. We'll have him back in no time."

Johnston looked uncomfortable, though she tried hard not to show it. It was a comment that made her feel like she was doing something underhanded. They finished their conversation, and Johnston left the office. Barnes set up everything involving the surveillance of the fourteen agents, while Johnston gathered up several analysts to find the connections that they needed. Once she did, she went back to her desk and sat down.

She took a deep breath, feeling conflicted. Why was she doing this? Was it to just help Holt? Or was it because it was her job to bring him back into the fold? And did it matter in either case? Part of her felt like she was doing something sinister. Like she was plotting this intricate, devilish plan to help Holt in order to reel him in. She hated that feeling. But she knew that was what was expected of her.

The only reason Barnes brought her into this was to bring Holt back. Nothing else had worked, so they figured they'd try the new person on him. And it appeared to be working so far. But she didn't want to just be some pawn in the game. She wanted to do things the right way.

Johnston put her elbows on her desk, balled her hands into fists, and placed them over her mouth and chin. Her eyes darted around the room as she watched people moving and working. They weren't frantic, but there was a definite haste in everyone's movements. Things had to be done quickly.

Her trance was interrupted by the sound of her phone. Startled, she picked it up off the desk and looked at the number. It wasn't anyone in her contact list.

"Johnston."

A man replied. "Your package will be ready tomorrow."

"Great. Where can he pick it up?"

"Have him meet me in Thailand. I'll be in Bangkok."

"I'm not sure he can get there tomorrow. He's traveling from Greece."

"Day after."

"OK. How will he know you?"

"Just give him my number when he gets there. We'll arrange a meet then."

"OK. I'll do that."

She barely got the words out of her mouth when the line went dead. She took the phone away from her ear and looked at it.

"All right, then."

She put the phone down and went back to her previous position of staring at everyone. This time, she only put her left hand over her face, covering her mouth. She went back to thinking about Holt. She wanted to do right by him. The man had just lost his wife, his world was spinning, and he needed to somehow find closure in all of this. And she had to help him so he didn't get killed in the process.

Suddenly, Johnston stood up, and grabbed her phone. She left the room, and proceeded to walk out of the building. She went into a small courtyard and found a seat at a round metal table. She sat there for a few minutes, watching a few of the trees, staring at the leaves rustle in the wind. She then dialed Holt's number. He immediately picked up.

"Got an update for you," Johnston said.

"Great. What is it?"

"It'll be ready the day after tomorrow. Well, it'll be ready tomorrow, but you'll have to travel a bit first."

"Where is it?"

"Bangkok. Thailand. The guy's already there."

"That's fine," Holt said. "I can get there."

"I'll send you his number. He said to contact him when you get there. You two can arrange a pickup when you arrive."

"Sounds good."

Johnston sighed. "Great. Um, I'll keep working on things."

Holt picked up on her voice. It was different. Not as upbeat-sounding as it usually was.

"So what's wrong?"

"Hmm? Nothing's wrong."

"I'm pretty good at reading people," Holt said. "And your voice is telling me something's bothering you."

"You have enough on your mind right now. Don't worry about my problems."

"I got a few minutes to listen."

"It's... it's nothing."

"Josie?"

"We really shouldn't talk about this, you know."

"It's about me, isn't it?"

"No. Yes. No. It's... it's really me. And you. And everything. I'm sorry. I'm not making sense."

"You sound conflicted about something," Holt said.

"It was... just something that Barnes mentioned to me. About reeling you in. And it just got me to thinking. I don't know why. Just one of those things that stick with you, I guess. For some reason."

"So what's the conflict?"

"Because I'm not sure why I'm doing this. I thought I was just doing this to help you. But Barnes expects this to lead somewhere. With you coming back. And I'm supposed to be the one doing that. So, am I really just saying I'm helping you with no expectations? Or am I really doing this with the ulterior motive of having you trust me and come back? I don't even know if I'm making sense. Or if this even matters. Or why I'm even telling you. This is probably only making things worse between us."

Holt chuckled. "It's not."

"Really? You're OK with everything I just said? I previously told you I only wanted to help you and that it didn't matter if you came back. Now, I'm not sure if I was actually lying to you. Maybe I'm in over my head with this. Maybe I should go back to my old position."

"No. You are good at this. You just don't know it yet."

"Between this and my boyfriend. Ex. I feel like my head is spinning sometimes."

"Join the club. But listen, it's impossible for you to help me out of the goodness of your heart with no expectations. You know why?"

"I'm sure you're going to tell me."

"Because we didn't just meet out of the blue. You were ordered to bring me back. So everything that happens after that is a byproduct of those orders."

"I'm sorry."

"You don't have to apologize. That's just the game that we're in. I'm fully aware of what Barnes wants. And you're trying to walk a tightrope of pleasing him and following your orders, and somehow convincing me to come back."

"I feel like I'm failing at both."

"You're not," Holt said. "Just do your job."

"If I just do my job, I feel like I'm deceiving you somehow."

"You know why you're the only person at the agency I'm talking to right now?"

"Because you feel sorry for me?"

Holt laughed. "Well, maybe a little. But the real reason is because when you tell me something, I believe it."

"You do?"

"For some reason. The moment I met you, I could tell there was something different about you."

"But, I'm still not helping you out of the goodness of my heart. I wanted to. But..."

"You're trying to make sense in a world that has a lot of gray in it. Josie, in this world that we live in, especially us, in this job, it's very difficult to do things out of the goodness of your heart. Everyone has an angle. Everyone has ulterior motives. You just understand that going in. Believe me, I have no misconceptions about why you're here. You want to help me. But you also want to do your job. If anything, what you told me makes me trust you more."

"Really?" Johnston said. "How so?"

"Because in real life, people have thoughts and fears, mixed emotions, and conflicts. They do things they shouldn't, think with their heart instead of their head, and sometimes vice versa. It's not a black-and-white world out there. Like I said, there's a lot of gray."

"I guess that's true."

"You know the people I don't trust?"

"Isn't it basically everyone?"

Holt laughed again. "Well, almost. But it's really the people that pretend they have all the answers. The ones that pretend there are no conflicts or mixed emotions. They have everything figured out. They're always certain. But that's bullshit. That's not life. And that's not human. We all question ourselves sometimes. Wonder why we went left instead of right. Why certain things bother us more than others. And sometimes it doesn't make any damn sense."

"That's for sure."

"But by you telling me all that, it lets me know you're a real person. You're not just an empty suit. You're not just going to tell me what I want to hear, regardless of how it affects me. You're willing to open up and be vulnerable. Those are the people that I trust. And believe me, in this line of work, you don't meet many."

Johnston let out another sigh. This one wasn't of frustration, though.

"Thanks for all that. It makes me feel better. I don't know why I was thinking all that. I guess I was just getting overwhelmed for a moment."

"Happens to everybody. That's why they say talking about it usually helps."

"You put me at ease. Thanks."

"No problem. I'm gonna have to go catch a plane. What was that number?"

Johnston told him. "Aaron?"

"Yeah?"

"Don't shut me out from here on out."

"What makes you think I would?"

"You could just get the new identity and passport and go to Singapore, straight to the White Horse Lounge, and wreck everything. Without letting me in."

"Yeah. I could."

"So let me help you. I am on your side."

"I know that," Holt replied.

"So don't charge in like you're a one-man brigade. Let me help you however I can."

"I will. And you should get back inside. You have work to do."

"How'd you know I was outside?"

"I can hear the wind blowing. And the leaves rustling."

"You're observant."

"Kind of my job."

"Yeah. Anyway, promise me you'll call me before you do anything?"

"I will, Josie. I promise."

They hung up, and Johnston smiled, thinking about the way he called her Josie. She was starting to get used to it. Maybe even liked it. She then hurried back inside the building. Feeling more confident about herself, she was determined to give Holt all the help he needed. No matter what.

22

It was around a 24-hour drive from Bangkok to Singapore. And when you were on a mission like Holt was, it seemed to take even longer. He picked up his new passport, complete with a new identity from the CIA contact in Bangkok. It went down without a hitch. He drove through Malaysia and just went through the Woodlands Checkpoint to get into Singapore. There seemed to be no complications.

It was about another twenty-minute drive to get to the White Horse Lounge. It was located in the middle of a strip center. Five other places surrounded it. On the surface, nothing looked unusual about it. Probably why they chose that location. It didn't stand out.

Parking was tight, even in the middle of the day. Holt just sat in his car and watched for a while. The place wasn't open just yet. Not for a few more hours. But he wanted to see who went in before then. Just as he promised he would, Holt called Johnston to let her know he was there. And that he hadn't gone in Rambo-style. She'd been waiting for his call and eagerly picked up on the first ring.

"Hey, you there?"

"Yeah. Just got here a few minutes ago."

"What are you doing right now?"

"Just watching," Holt answered.

"Good. Because you're gonna need to find a different way in."

"Why?"

"I did some digging. Nobody gets in there uninvited. You need to have a pass."

"Can you get me one?"

"I don't know what they look like. I just know you need one. Some type of ID card. And there are bouncers at the door checking."

"That really doesn't concern me."

"Well it should," Johnston said. "If you decide to go in the hard way, by the time you figure out where you're going, the people you're after will be long gone. You're The Nobody Man. You blend in. You go unnoticed. That's the man you need to be right now. No one else."

Holt let her words sink in. She was right. No matter how deep his hatred burned, this wasn't the time for that. He had to be the man he used to be.

"So how do you get an invite to this place?"

"You either have to know someone, or you have to be invited," Johnston replied.

"We can strike both of those off the list."

"Or an employee."

Holt sighed. "I think they'll notice someone new coming in and making drinks."

"You don't have to go into that lounge, you know. If it's not happening, it's not happening. You don't have to force it. We can find these guys where they live or somewhere else."

"That's being passive. One at a time. The first one goes down, everyone else might rabbit. I need to get them all at once."

"You don't even know if they're all going to be in there. You could make a grand entrance just for nothing."

"I have to strike before they know what hits them. Once they know I'm coming, they'll have too much time to prepare. And the spot they would expect the least is inside that building."

"I don't see how you're going to do that unless you sneak in through an air vent or something."

Holt's attention perked up as he saw someone exit the building. It obviously was someone who worked there. But it sparked an idea. He didn't need to break his way in, or fabricate an entrance. He just needed an ID card. It just wouldn't be his.

"I got it."

"What?" Johnston asked.

"I'm just gonna sit here all night until I find someone."

"And do what with them?"

"Steal their card."

"Who exactly are you looking for?"

"I don't know. I think it's one of those I'll know it when I find it type of deals."

"What if you don't find it?"

"I will," Holt said.

"All right, well, I guess let me know if you need something. I'll keep at it."

Holt continued to sit in the same spot for several hours. The lounge opened up at five. There weren't a lot of customers going in at open. A few. Most of the activity didn't start happening until seven. All the men were dressed in suits. Not one person deviated. All the women were in dresses. Some were short, some were long, some showed plenty of skin, some didn't show much at all. But it was obvious this place had a specific dress code. And right now, Holt didn't fit in. But he would by the time he came back the next time.

Holt didn't deviate from that spot until about ten. That was when people started to leave, though there were still plenty of people just getting there. The lounge didn't close until two in the morning. Holt focused on every person that left. He didn't know what he was looking for. He figured it would just jump out at him when he saw it.

Finally, one man caught Holt's attention as he

exited the White Horse Lounge. He was tall, and dressed impeccably in a tailored suit, his posture exuding confidence and authority. He was probably in his mid-40's, and carrying a briefcase. There was just something that stuck out about him. Maybe it was the briefcase. And he was alone. Most people that went into the lounge went in with someone else. And the fact that he was carrying a briefcase indicated some type of business dealing. Now knowing what kind of front the White Horse Lounge was used for, Holt figured maybe that business was something he needed to stick his nose in.

Holt watched as the man casually lit a cigarette, his eyes scanning the street before he started walking towards a sleek black car parked nearby. This was the guy. Holt started his car, and waited for the other man to start driving. He kept a safe distance while on the road to avoid raising suspicion. They drove for about twenty minutes, before the car finally pulled in front of a house.

Holt stopped and pulled over to the side of the road as he watched the man enter the property. It was a contemporary style house. Four bedrooms, a square, in-ground pool in the back, and about five-thousand square feet of space. This was obviously a man who'd done very well for himself.

There was a large concrete wall that surrounded the property. Holt was going to have to figure out a way over it. As he circled the perimeter, he noticed a section of the wall that seemed to be partially hidden by overgrown bushes. It was his way in.

Under the cover of darkness, Holt made his move. He leapt up and grasped the top of the wall, pulling himself up and over with practiced ease. He landed on the other side in a crouch, scanning his surroundings for any immediate threats. There was nothing but darkness.

Holt crept towards the house, sticking to the shadows as he approached a side window. As he got closer, he could hear faint strains of music drifting through the air. Classical. He took a look through the sliding glass doors in front of the pool. He observed the man leaving the room to go into another.

The man reappeared again, and headed straight for the sliding glass doors. He was on the phone and opened them, stepping outside. Holt disappeared behind a wall. With the man engaged in conversation, he walked near the pool and stood next to it. His back was to the house.

Holt quickly darted into the house before the man turned around. He hurriedly went into another room, finding a closet that he could duck into. There were some men who wouldn't go to all this trouble. A less experienced person, or one who embraced the violence, might have just put a bullet in this guy's head when he wasn't looking, then took what they wanted.

But Holt didn't operate that way. Not when he didn't know anything about this guy. He might've been

The Nobody Man

a banker for all Holt knew. Besides, killing always brought questions. It brought visibility. It brought heat. And right now, Holt wanted to be invisible. Nobody could know he was there. They couldn't even suspect it. That meant he couldn't do anything to raise even the slightest suspicion that he could be around. So he'd wait until the right time.

After a few minutes, the man came back into the house and closed the sliding doors. He made a quick trip to the kitchen, then made his way to his bedroom. Holt could hear the shower turn on. This was the time to make a move.

Holt exited the closet, then started looking around for the man's wallet. He figured the ID card would be in there. Most people kept their wallets or purses in the same places. Kitchen counters, a shelf in a living room, or maybe on the dresser in their bedroom. Very few people deviated from the usual spots.

This person was no different. Once Holt checked the kitchen, he saw the man's wallet and keys on the end of the counter. Holt hurried over to it and started rifling through it. He noticed the driver's license, and some credit cards, then saw another card. This one had no writing on it. It only had a logo in the bottom left corner. It was the head of a white horse, with a circle around it. This was what he was looking for.

Holt stuck it in his pocket, then moved back through the house. As he did, he noticed the briefcase on the table between a couch and the TV. His instincts told him he needed to take a peek inside. He needed to see what this guy was up to. Whether he was legit or not.

Holt went over to the couch and opened the briefcase. It appeared to be nothing but real estate contracts. Holt quickly scanned through dozens of pages, though nothing struck him as out of the ordinary. He figured the man was probably at the lounge discussing a business deal with someone. Maybe it wasn't on the up-and-up. But nothing Holt was looking at made it seem so. And he wasn't going to stay there any longer to investigate. The guy seemed clean at first glance, and that was good enough for him. If something was fishy, he'd sent the info to Johnston and let her check him out. Right now, it didn't seem necessary.

Holt quickly exited outside through the sliding glass doors again. He ran until he reached the same spot in the wall he climbed over initially. Seconds later, he was back over the wall again, hurrying to his car. He hopped in and sped off. As he drove, he pulled out the ID card and looked at it. A smile crept over his face. Now he was in business.

23

Holt arrived back at the White Horse Lounge around midnight. Without knowing what the layout was inside, he was going in unarmed. It was a slight risk. If The Black Phoenix somehow knew he was there, he was giving them an easier target. But Johnston was right. He couldn't go in there with the intention of causing havoc and destruction just yet. He had to be sure about what he was doing. And right now, there were too many unanswered questions.

Holt found another spot to park, though this time was further away. There still were a lot of cars around, even at that time of night. He waited until another couple started walking towards the doors. He quickly got in line behind them. He'd study their movements on the way in.

There was a man in a suit on the door. No doubt a bouncer. He opened the door for all of them and smiled as they passed. Now standing in a vestibule, Holt noticed two more men standing by another door. They were also dressed in suits. Tough-looking. There was also a metal detector everyone passed through. Once they did that, there was a card reader on the wall next to the door. Holt slid his ID card in, and as soon as the light flashed green, he was good to go.

He glanced at the guard to his right, who simply nodded at him, letting him know he could go in. Holt pushed the door open and went inside.

The lounge was dimly lit, with plush red velvet seating and a long mahogany bar. The murmur of conversation filled the air, punctuated by the clinking of glasses and soft jazz music playing in the background. Holt scanned the room, his eyes darting from table to table. It mostly looked like couples enjoying a night out together.

Holt found an empty seat at the bar and ordered a scotch, surveying the room discreetly. He spotted a corner booth where a group of men were engaged in hushed conversation. One of them had a distinct air of authority, exuding power and control. Holt's instincts told him that this might be someone of interest. As he continued to casually watch, he noticed one of them had a distinctive tattoo on his forearm. A black phoenix in flight.

As Holt sipped his drink, he noticed a figure approaching him from the corner of his eye. It was an Asian woman, dressed elegantly in a form-fitting black dress that accentuated her curves. She took a seat next to Holt at the bar, her eyes flickering with curiosity as she studied him.

"You're not from around here, are you?" she asked in a smooth voice that hinted at hidden depths.

"What gives it away?"

She smiled knowingly, her gaze unwavering. "I have a good eye for strangers in this town. And you, my friend, have an air of mystery about you."

Her words hung in the air, charged with unspoken questions. In most situations, Holt would have shooed the woman away, not wanting to have any distractions. But in this environment, it almost seemed better that he was seen with someone. A man alone there seemed out of place.

Holt returned her smile with a nod of acknowledgment. "And what about you? Are you a regular in this establishment?"

The woman chuckled softly, a melodic sound that seemed to blend with the ambient jazz music. "Let's just say I know my way around here. And I have a knack for spotting those who don't quite fit in."

"Buy you a drink?"

The woman smiled. "I thought you'd never ask."

Holt motioned to the bartender. "Bring something for the lady?"

The bartender nodded, coming down with a drink in almost no time. Holt and the woman touched glasses, then both took sips of their drinks. As the woman put her drink down on the bar, her eyes glanced over him with a mixture of curiosity and assessment.

She spoke in a low, melodic voice, "You're not here for the drinks or the ambiance, are you?"

Holt turned to face her, his expression guarded but attentive. "Depends on what you think I'm here for," he replied, taking another sip of his scotch.

The woman smiled knowingly, revealing a hint of dimples on her cheeks. "I think you're here for answers." She then whispered cryptically. "And maybe a little trouble."

"What kind of trouble?"

She seductively looked at him. "I wish it was the kind that involved me. But I know that's not what you're here for, is it?"

"Oh? Why don't you think that is?"

"You have a ring on your finger for one. And you don't strike me as the type to step out."

Holt glanced down at his hand. "No, I'm not."

"So, what's a nice guy like you doing in a place like this, then? I doubt it's for pleasure. That means it must be business."

Holt raised an eyebrow, intrigued. "You seem to know a lot about me for someone I've never met before."

She chuckled softly, her eyes gleaming with amusement. "Let's just say I have a keen sense for people who don't belong. You stick out like a sore thumb in this establishment, Mr. Holt."

Holt's eyes immediately bulged, surprised at hearing his name, though he tried to play it off. "Who?"

The woman leaned in closer, her voice barely above a whisper. "Relax, Mr. Holt." She then slowly put her arms around his neck as if they were being intimate, putting her face next to his. "Your reputation precedes you, especially in certain circles. I know who you are and why you're here."

Holt's jaw tensed slightly, his eyes narrowing as he studied the woman beside him. "And what exactly do you know about me?"

She smirked, a glint of mischief in her eyes. "I know you're not just a tourist passing through. You're here on a mission, one that involves a certain group that prefers to keep their activities under the radar."

Holt pulled away, their faces just inches away from each other. "What makes you think you don't have the wrong guy?"

"We have friends in the same places."

"I doubt that."

"OK. Let's just say we have mutual acquaintances, then."

Holt's mind immediately raced to Florakis. It had to be him. Nobody else knew he was coming here, other than the CIA, and he figured they didn't leak it. But Florakis knew.

Holt's grip tightened on his glass, his mind racing with possibilities. Was she friend or foe? Could he trust her? He took a sip of his drink.

"How do I know you're not working for them?"

A devilish grin formed on the woman's face and she reached out to touch his hand lightly.

"If I were working for them, we wouldn't be having this conversation. You would already be dead. Trust me when I say I'm on your side."

"How'd you know I was going to be here?"

"So many questions." She turned her head and saw the dance floor, where there were several other couples slow-dancing already. "We should blend in as much as possible."

Holt looked over at the dance floor, not really feeling it. But the woman grabbed his hand and led him over there. Holt didn't resist. The woman instantly pressed her body against his, each putting their arms around the other. Holt was mildly uncomfortable with the arrangement.

She whispered in his ear. "We have to make it look good."

"Who are you?"

"You can call me Hana."

"You didn't tell me how you knew I'd be here."

"I was told you visited a certain person in Greece. You were given a list of names. Assuming you'd want to take those names out, it was logical you'd come here in a day or two. After you figured out how you'd arrive undetected."

"Seems like you have all the answers."

"In this business, people who don't have all the answers get killed. I first got here yesterday in case you showed up."

"So what's your stake in this?"

"Just a job."

"You were hired?"

"Well I'm not doing it out of the goodness of my heart."

"Florakis?"

"I don't think names are necessary, do you?"

"So what are you here for?"

"To make sure you're able to do what you're here for."

"I don't like surprises," Holt said.

"Few people in our business do."

"So what exactly is your job here?"

"To make sure you're able to do yours. As efficiently as possible."

Hana guided Holt with practiced steps on the dance floor, their movements fluid and seemingly intimate to any onlookers. Holt couldn't shake off the feeling of being out of his element, but he followed Hana's lead, trying to blend in with the other dancers.

"So what can you tell me that will help in that endeavor?"

Hana turned her head to the corner of the room. At

the table Holt had previously identified which had the man with the tattoo.

"See those four men at the corner table?"

Holt's eyes went in that direction. "One man has a Black Phoenix tattoo on his arm."

"All four work here. Security."

They slow-danced their way to a different position, turning their bodies to the side.

"Door to our left," Hana said. "Man standing next to it."

Holt glanced at it out of the corner of his eye. "Yeah?"

"Leads to the upstairs offices. There's a long hallway. Five doors on each side."

"Seems like you did a lot of work in one night."

"It's not that hard to get information if you know the right words to say. And how to move your assets."

"I can imagine."

"A little alcohol, a little skin, and a few dirty words… you can get most men eating out of your hand if you want."

"So what else can you tell me?"

"The three men you're looking for aren't here."

"So where are they?" Holt asked.

"Right now, I have no idea. They'll be here tomorrow, though."

"How can you be sure?"

"There's a meeting from what I can tell."

"How good's your source?"

"The guy with the Black Phoenix tattoo on his arm?"

"Yeah?"

"He told me. There was a lot of liquor involved."

"And he wasn't the least bit suspicious of your questions?"

"I doubt he remembers anything except a hard night of drinking and partying," Hana answered. "One of the benefits of slipping a little white pill into a champagne glass undetected. He probably only barely remembers his own name today."

"Any idea on the time of the meeting?"

"Think it's happening at nine."

"All five main players?"

"Think it's just the three that are around here."

"Know what they're discussing?" Holt asked.

"No. Doesn't really matter, does it?"

"Not really."

"From what I know, once we get through that door with the guard, there will be two more guards standing in the hallway outside the meeting room."

"What are the other rooms up there?"

"There's two rooms with some dancing females putting on a show for whoever's watching. It's an extra fee to get up there."

"What kind of dancing?"

"The kind without clothes. Why, you interested in attending?"

"No. What else?"

"There are a couple of other private rooms for other purposes. More intimate purposes. If you're interested, I could try to book one for us."

"No thanks."

"Still devoted to your wife even though she's not around?" Hana could feel Holt's fingers tighten up on her body. "I apologize if that was disrespectful. I didn't mean it as such."

"It's fine."

"I know why you're here. I respect that."

"Let's just stick to business. There are metal detectors outside. How am I going to get up there?"

"How are *we* going to get up there, you mean?"

"I thought you were only here to provide information?"

"I'm here to provide whatever you need. I figure tomorrow, we can book one of those rooms up there. Then we do whatever needs to be done."

"With what weapons? As I mentioned, there are metal detectors on the door."

"I was under the impression you didn't need a gun to kill."

"I don't. It's just easier. Especially with two guards on the door, and three men inside. Plus, whoever needs to be dealt with on the way out if things get hairy."

"Don't worry. I've got you covered."

"How?" Holt asked.

"A girl's gotta keep a few secrets, doesn't she?"

"Not when it's my life on the line."

"The kitchen staff comes through the back door," Hana replied. "They're patted down on the way in. But boxes that come in are not as exhaustively searched. Especially food and alcohol."

"I take it you've got a solution?"

Hana gazed into his eyes, rubbing the back of his head. Their noses were touching. She really wanted to kiss him, though she respected his intentions.

"I made friends with one of the cook's last night."

"You were busy."

"No time to waste, right?"

"He agreed to bring in a couple boxes of champagne. Underneath will be a few handguns. The boxes aren't inspected so intensely. The guns will get through."

"And what's he getting for this generous help?"

"A nice payday," Hana answered. "About six months worth of work for one small action."

"And how will we get them?"

"The bathroom is right next to the kitchen. Tomorrow night, I'll go to the bathroom. On the way back, I'll slip into the kitchen. He'll have the guns in a box next to the door underneath some empty bottles. Then we'll go upstairs. How's that sound?"

"Sounds like a plan."

Hana grinned. "I was hoping you'd say that."

"I should probably get out of here before anyone gets suspicious."

"We should leave together. It'll look better."

They took their hands off each other and started walking toward the door. Hana then slipped her hand in Holt's.

"Play the part."

Though Holt was uneasy about holding another woman's hand, he didn't let it go. Appearances mattered in places like this. Once they went outside, he let go of Hana's hand.

"Aren't you going to walk me to my car?"

Holt stiffened his jaw, but walked next to her. She took his arm and put it around her.

"They have cameras out here, you know."

"I saw," Holt said.

"Just pretend you can't keep your hands off me."

"We don't need to take it that far."

They walked together until they reached her car. She stopped and turned toward him, putting her arms around him again.

"I assume you wouldn't want to stop at my hotel for a nightcap?"

"I don't think so."

"Too bad. We could have a great time."

"Seems like you don't need me for that."

Hana smirked. She then kissed him on the cheek. "See you soon."

24

Once Holt got back to his hotel, he called Johnston. There was a thirteen hour time difference between them, so even though it was past two in the morning in Singapore, she was in the middle of her workday.

"How'd you night go?"

"Eventful," Holt replied. "Not in the way I initially hoped, though."

"What happened?"

"Targets aren't there. Tomorrow."

"Oh. Well, gives you extra time to prepare, I guess."

"Not sure it's needed. That's what I'm calling about. I met someone while I was there. A woman."

"Oh. Well, you know, you don't really need to tell me about all that."

"Not in that way."

"Oh. OK. Then what?"

"Her name is Hana. Or so she said. I got the feeling she was either hired by Florakis, or is working with him."

"For what purpose?"

"To help me, apparently. She said her job was to make sure I was able to do mine. She knew who I was and what I was there for."

"Where'd this happen?"

"Inside the club," Holt answered.

"A little concerning."

"I'd say. She said she's able to sneak weapons inside the building for tomorrow. Apparently, that's when the next meeting is taking place with our subjects."

"And what is she getting out of this?"

"Beats me. I guess just a paycheck."

"What do you want me to do?" Johnston asked.

"I'd like you to run her. Find out as much about her as possible. I want to know exactly who I'm dealing with. And whether I can trust her."

"Well, I'd say no to that last part already. I wouldn't trust anyone who just shows up unannounced."

"Isn't that what you did?"

"Beg your pardon?"

"Didn't you just show up to me unannounced?"

"Uh, well, that's different in my case."

"Why is it?"

"Because… because I wasn't… you know."

Holt laughed. "Right."

"It is!"

"If you say so."

"Anyway, do you have this woman's last name?"

"Nope. Can't you access cameras or something to run facial recognition on it?"

"Not on the White Horse cameras, I can't. We've already tried. They've got top-notch encryption."

"I guess that stands to reason, considering who they are. What about other cameras nearby?"

"Yeah, I can start checking. What's this woman look like?"

"5'5, 5'6, Asian, long black hair, pretty, average weight."

"I'll start running it now. Might take some time."

"That's all right. It'll give me some time to catch up on some sleep."

"You OK?" Johnston asked.

Holt sighed. "Yeah. Just tired."

"I didn't mean physically. I mean… are *you* OK?"

Holt knew what she was referring to. And he honestly wasn't sure. He didn't have time to grieve like most people would. He could have. Maybe if Denise's death were under normal circumstances. But they weren't. There really wasn't time to reflect, or think, or go into some deep, dark spiral. He immediately went into full-time revenge mode. Maybe when this was all over, he'd crawl into the bottom of a bottle, or sit in the corner of a room for days and cry his eyes out. But he just couldn't afford to do that now. Not with what was at stake.

"I'm OK."

"I don't believe you," Johnston said. "You wouldn't be the man that I think you are if you were."

Holt quickly wiped his eyes. It was lucky they couldn't see each other, so she couldn't see his eyes getting red.

"I'm getting through the days. It probably helps that I have a purpose. A reason to keep going. If not... I dunno."

"I know you're probably not someone who's ever going to do this, but... I'll throw it out there. If you ever need a shoulder or an ear... I'm here."

"Thanks. But you're right. I probably won't."

"I figured as much. But the offer still stands. And that's from me. Not the agency."

"Thank you. When this is over, maybe I'll take the time to let it hit me. But right now, I can't afford to. At this moment, I just need to get a few hours of sleep and I'll be fine. Feel like I've been running around non-stop for the past week."

"That's because you have. Ever since... well, you've just been flying from one place to another, going to different places, getting into conflicts... at some point you'll have to slow down."

"When this is over. If I slow down before then, it gives them all a chance to get away. I've gotta press."

"I know. I just don't want you to run yourself down and make a mistake because your body's tired."

"I'll be fine. I've done a lot worse than this. I'm not even close to being on fumes."

"Would you tell me if you were?"

"Probably not."

Johnston laughed. "Well, at least you're honest."

"I'm good. Few hours of sleep and I'll be where I need to be. I won't make a mistake with this much on the line. Unless it concerns Hana."

"What exactly is your concern if it seems like she's helping?"

"I've been in this business long enough to know that your friend today could be your enemy tomorrow. Especially if the payday is large enough. How do I know if her job is to help me get in and eliminate these threats, then I let my guard down, and she eliminates me right after?"

"I see your point. Your trust issues again, right?"

"If you'd have seen and experienced half the things I have, you'd have trust issues too."

"I have no doubt of that," Johnston said. "OK. I'm gonna go and see what I can dig up on this Hana woman. You get some sleep. Call me when you wake up and I'll let you know what I got. If anything."

"You'll have something."

"What makes you so sure?"

"Because if you come up empty, then this woman

kills me after helping me, you'll feel bad about yourself."

"Oh, gee, thanks. Way to guilt-trip me."

Holt chuckled. "Just figured I'd up the stakes a little."

"Wow. No pressure or anything."

"Hey, just figured I'd give you some extra motivation."

"I really didn't need any of that kind, you know."

"Never hurts."

"Anyway, I *will* make sure I have something for you whenever you wake up. Try to get at least six hours, though."

"Why six?"

"Because I have a feeling I'll need every minute you can give me."

"OK. Will do. Should we synchronize watches?"

"Don't be ridiculous."

"OK. I'll call you later."

"Sleep well." They hung up, and Johnston put her phone down on the desk. She took a deep sigh. "No pressure."

Johnston got up and went to the desk of another analyst, letting him know what she needed. He immediately got to work on it. Within twenty minutes, he had footage of Holt and Hana together. They were standing near her car outside the White Horse Lounge. Luckily for them, the parking was tight, and she parked further away. The camera that picked them up was from a nearby business.

"Zoom in on her," Johnston said.

Once they got a better look at her, they cropped her face and put it through the facial recognition software. While they waited for the results, Johnston went back to her desk and continued working. Several hours passed before the software finished its pass. The analyst came back over to Johnston's desk. She looked up at him, hope plainly evident on her face. He just shook his head at her.

"Scan's finished. Nothing popped."

Her shoulders instantly slumped. "What do you mean? Nothing?"

"Didn't get a single hit."

"How can that be?"

"We must have her on file somewhere."

The analyst shrugged. "All I can tell you is that nothing popped."

Johnston closed her eyes and put her hand on her head in frustration. "All right, thanks."

He handed her the photo of Hana. She stared at the woman, wondering how she fit into all of this. Johnston didn't want to have another conversation with Holt in a few hours and tell him they had nothing. She had to find out something about Hana. Johnston continued staring at the photo, as if something would magically pop out at her.

"Who are you?"

25

Johnston continuously looked at the clock, then at her phone, wondering when it was going to ring. It was seven, and in most cases, she would've gone home for the day by now. It was eight in the morning in Singapore. She had knots in her stomach, feeling like she was letting Holt down. She felt like a failure. She didn't want to tell him that she'd come up with nothing. He needed her to tell him whether Hana was a person he could trust, and she couldn't do it.

She put her hands over her face, dreading that phone ringing. She wished she had something for him. Anything. But she didn't. Not one single thing.

Then Johnston was startled, jumping slightly, when the phone finally did ring. She looked at the ID. It was Holt. She closed her eyes for a second and took a deep breath. She picked it up and accepted the call. She put the phone up to her ear, though she didn't mutter a word. Uncomfortable with the silence, Holt spoke up.

"Josie?"

"Hi. I'm here."

It was plainly evident in her voice that something was wrong. There was no mistaking that.

"What's the problem?"

She didn't want to say it. "Um. Well... it's, um..."

Holt could tell she was nervous about something. He figured it was either one of two things. She was about to tell him Hana was the most lethal person ever invented, and that he couldn't trust her as far as he could throw her. And that she'd definitely kill him when the time was right. Or, she couldn't tell him anything about her. He guessed the latter. If it was the former, he assumed Johnston's tone of voice would be different. Right now, she sounded defeated. If it was the other thing, he believed there would have been a sense of urgency in her voice, and she'd come right out with it. Now, she was stalling. Not intentionally. Just because she felt badly about it.

Johnston sighed. "Listen, we tried to... we..."

Holt couldn't let her twist in the wind like that. If it was someone he didn't like, maybe. He'd probably give them as long a leash as possible. But he liked her. Not in the romantic way. He just felt like she was a good person who tried to do the right thing.

"You couldn't find anything on her, could you?"

Johnston was silent for a moment. Then she cleared her throat.

"You know, we tried everything we could. We, um..."

Holt let out a laugh. "Josie, it's OK."

"No, it's not. I'm sorry. You were counting on me to find something on this woman and I... I couldn't do it. I failed. And I'm sorry. I just..."

"Josie."

"Yeah?"

"It's OK. I'm not surprised you came up with nothing."

"You are?"

"I knew there was a chance when I told you about her," Holt said. "I just figured it was worth the shot."

"I'm sorry."

"Stop apologizing. I know you did everything possible. That's the business. Sometimes these things happen. There will always be wrinkles, and things that pop up out of nowhere. Surprises. Sometimes you can account for them. Sometimes you can't. This is one of those wild cards."

"I just feel like I let you down."

"You didn't."

"We checked everything," Johnston said. "Facial rec, passports, ID's, everything. Her face just didn't pop up."

"Like I said, it's not surprising. She strikes me as someone who's very, very good. And she knows it. And you don't get like that by being some run-of-the-mill slob."

"Like you?"

"Did you just call me a run-of-the-mill slob?"

Johnston's eyes almost popped out, realizing how it came across. "Oh, no, no, no. No, I didn't mean it like that! I meant the other part, not the slob part. The very, very, good part. Oh my, I'm sorry."

Holt had a good chuckle at her expense. "Wow. Insulting me already."

"No, I really didn't mean that. I promise. I... just wanna go home and crawl into bed already."

Holt continued laughing. "It's fine. I know what you meant."

Johnston put her hand on her head. "I think I need some aspirin."

"Josie, it's OK. I'm just kidding with you. I know how you meant it. We're good."

"I can stay here and keep working on it until I find something."

"Isn't it like seven there?"

"Yeah."

"Go home," Holt said. "Relax. Get some rest. That meeting is at nine tonight. That's eight your time. Right when you get into the office."

"I'll probably get in early in case you need me for something beforehand. Maybe I'll get in at seven."

"You don't have to."

"I want to be there for you if you need me."

"Thanks."

"Especially since I didn't..."

Holt knew what she was about to say and wanted to put a stop to it right then and there. He didn't want her feeling bad about herself. In their business, sometimes information was elusive. It was all part of the game. She had to understand that and not take it personally. There were plenty of things in the game to take personally. But this wasn't one of them.

"Don't do that."

"What?"

"Beat yourself up over this," Holt answered. "It happens."

"How are you going to protect yourself against her?"

"Believe me, this isn't the first time I've worked with people I didn't trust. Or know. I'll just do what I always do. Keep a close eye on her."

"How are you going to do that if things get chaotic? What if you have to turn your back to her? What if you lose her in a crowd of gunfire? What then?"

"Pray that my fears are unfounded."

"That's not a strategy."

"Didn't say it was."

"Maybe... maybe we should hold off on this."

"No," Holt replied. "The meeting is tonight. Three of them will be there. We can cut off the head of this thing."

"I just don't want it to be your head that's cut off."

"There are always risks. Very rarely is there a perfect mission. You just have to mitigate the risks as much as possible."

"And do you think that's possible here?"

"I'll make it work."

Johnston was silent again, but Holt detected a small noise she made with her mouth. She probably didn't mean to. It was just one of those reflex actions people made without thinking about it.

"What else?"

"Hmm?"

"Is there something else on your mind?" Holt asked.

"Oh, um, no... I guess not."

"Josie? If you have something on your mind, I'd like you to tell me."

"I, uh... I'm not sure if I should say."

"Why not?"

"I'm not sure how you'll take it."

"I think our relationship is getting off to a good start. I'd rather not ruin it by keeping secrets or holding things back. If it's important enough to go through your mind, it's important enough to tell me. Whatever it is, I can take it."

"It's just... you've been gone for three years."

"I'm aware."

"And now you're going back into this head-on like no time has passed at all. I don't mean to imply that you're... not as good as you used to be. But what if you're just rusty? Or..."

"What you're really wondering is if I've lost something."

"I'm sorry, I don't mean to..."

"Would you stop apologizing? I wouldn't respect you if you kept things like this to yourself."

"I'm sorry, it's... oh, I did it again. I'm sorry... no, I'm... I'm just gonna stop talking."

"Look, you're right to question it. And I don't ever want you to stop. People die out here all the time because they think they have all the answers, even when they don't. Sometimes the truth hurts. Sometimes you don't want to hear it. But that doesn't mean it shouldn't be said. Especially between us. And that doesn't mean I'll always agree, or not get mad, but I'll always listen."

"A lot of time has passed. And you're not just walking into some biker hangout here. These are professional killers."

"So am I."

"You were. Time and situations can change that. I'm not saying you should stop, I'm just saying... maybe this isn't the time or place?"

"It has to be now," Holt replied. "If not now, then when?"

"When it's a more advantageous position?"

"Which might not ever come. Or if they get spooked and they're gone for good. I can't let this go."

"I didn't actually expect you would. I just want you to be careful and... maybe improvise if you're a little rusty."

"You know, I wondered about that too."

"What?"

"Like you said, three years is a long time. And it's not like I was doing things during that time to keep my skills sharp. I was basically a homebody. Taking care of my wife and dog. I wasn't sure, myself. But in those alleys in Sicily, it all came back to me. It was just second nature. I didn't have to think. It just came to me. Reflex. They were as strong as ever."

"And when you get into that building?"

"I'll do what I have to. More than anything, the will to fight and to keep going is why I will prevail. I have to bring those responsible for killing my wife to justice. I *have* to. There is no alternative, no other option, no other outcome. Because there is more to do after this. It doesn't stop here. If I lose here, they win. And I cannot let that happen. I *won't* let that happen."

"Well, I can't be there with you to help. But I can be here to help. Whatever you need. Before and after, I'll be here."

"There is something you can do to help," Holt said. "It's going to be instrumental."

"What is it?"

"After tonight, there are two more targets to get. At least as far as the leadership is concerned."

"Yeah?"

"And once they hear about this, who knows how they'll react? Could tighten up security so much it's impenetrable. They could just go into hiding. But they'll do something."

"So what do you want me to do?"

"You need to get me out of Singapore and into Hong Kong as quickly as possible. No breaks. Once the next guy hears what happened, I don't know. That's why I need to get there before they find out. And it'll be in the middle of the night. So it's all the better. I can use that to my advantage. I'll worry about the White Horse Lounge. You worry about everything after."

"OK. Yeah. I can do that. It's about three hours from Singapore to Hong Kong. And then another three hours from Hong Kong to Tokyo."

"So everything can be wrapped up before the sun comes up."

"Well, I don't know about that, but... we can try."

"Josie? I'm counting on you for this."

"I'll make it happen. I promise. I'll get you to Hong Kong quickly. Just be ready to move."

"No worries about that. I'm ready."

26

Holt arrived at the White Horse Lounge around eight o'clock. Parking was already tight, and he had to find a spot further away from the building than he would have liked. As he walked to the building, he made a quick call to Johnston.

"Hey," she greeted. "How ya doing?"

"Just wanted to let you know I'm on my way in now."

"I'm ready when you get out."

"What's the plan?"

"Private plane. Waiting for you at the airport. You just have to get there."

"About thirty minutes from here," Holt said.

"Does that work for you?"

"Yeah. You're sure it's going to be there?"

"Positive. It's already there. Just waiting for you."

"Am I on a time limit?"

"No. It'll stay there until you arrive."

As he got closer to the building, Holt noticed Hana standing up against the side of the wall. She was just waiting for him.

"I see Hana. I gotta go."

"Aaron?"

"Yeah?"

"Be careful," Johnston said.

"Always."

Holt put his phone in his pocket as he reached Hana's position. She looked beautiful. Her hair was flowing past her shoulders, she had makeup on, and a dress on that would turn every man's head. And some women too. She had on a revealing blue dress that went down to her feet, though it had a high slit up the side of her thigh on her left leg. Holt was dressed in a regular suit. Nothing fancy about it. But it passed the dress code. Hana stood up straight as Holt reached her, almost flaunting herself at him. She had a flirty grin on her face.

"You look nice," Holt said.

"I was hoping for a little bit more than that."

"We're here on business, remember?"

"Oh, I'm painfully aware."

"Maybe when this is over, we can have that nightcap?"

"Can't. After this is over, I have more business elsewhere."

"Ah. Hong Kong, maybe?"

Holt just glared at her. "Am I going to happen to see you there?"

Hana shook her head. "Not me. I'm only contracted for this job."

"And why is that?"

She shrugged. "I don't know. Maybe this is considered the toughest assignment. Maybe it was assumed you didn't need help with the rest. I'm only told what I need to know. Should we go in?"

Holt looked at his watch. "We still have some time. Before we do, I want to make something clear."

"Oh? What's that?"

"You better not cross me."

"You don't trust me?"

"I don't trust anyone I don't know."

Hana put her hands on his chest. "Well, if you would've come to my hotel last night, you could've gotten to know me very well."

Holt took her hands off him. "I'm serious."

"You don't have to be concerned about me. If I was hired to kill you, we wouldn't even be here. I could've alerted people to your presence last night. I could've jumped you myself, and not in the good way."

"I just want to make sure we're on the same page here."

"We are," Hana replied. "Believe me, I've heard your reputation. You are one person I don't want for an enemy."

"What's your last name, by the way?"

Hana smirked, then put her finger on his lips. "Another time, maybe. We have work to do."

She walked away, headed towards the door of the building. Holt quickly caught up to her. They interlocked arms, putting on the facade of being together. The guard at the door opened it for them as they walked through it. They then went through the metal detectors and put their ID cards against the device. Once it went green, the doors were opened for them. They went inside, where it was already bustling with activity. It was much busier than the night before. There had to already be about two hundred people in there. And there were more coming behind them.

"More people, better for us," Hana said.

Holt nodded as he looked around. "Yeah."

"Let's grab a table so we don't look out of place."

They found one that had a view of the side door that went to the second floor. They didn't know if Kwon and the others would be walking through the front door, or if they had their own special entrance. Hana sat down gracefully, crossing her legs and scanning the room. Holt took the seat across from her, his posture relaxed yet alert. The two of them made quite the striking pair. Hana exuded elegance and charm, while Holt emanated power and determination. They exchanged a few quiet words as they observed the crowd, noting the various groups of people mingling around the lounge.

As they waited, a waiter approached their table to

take their drink orders. Hana ordered a glass of champagne, while Holt opted for a simple scotch on the rocks. The minutes ticked by slowly, tension mounting with each passing second. After twenty minutes had passed, Hana's eyes darted towards the side door as a group of well-dressed individuals entered the lounge. Among them was Kwon, unmistakable with his confident stride and air of authority.

"They're here," Hana whispered.

Holt looked over, watching the group as they maneuvered through the room. They didn't stop or slow down, or even mingle with anyone. They made a beeline straight for that side door. The guard opened it up as Kwon and his entourage made their way through. Besides Kwon, there were the two other leaders of The Black Phoenix. And there were six guards around them, who also went up to the second floor.

"Nine," Holt said. "Not including anyone else who may be up there already."

Hana glanced up at some cameras in the corner of the room. "Probably a security or surveillance room up there."

They kept their eyes on that side door as a couple other patrons went over to it. They had to scan their ID cards at the door, and present what looked like a ticket stub to the guard before he let anyone pass.

"That might be challenging," Holt said.

Hana reached into her purse and put Holt's ticket

on the table. "We've got the room with the King-sized bed."

Holt glanced at the ticket, then at her. "Should we get started?"

Hana smiled. "I thought you'd never ask." She stood up, giving Holt a seductive look. "I'll be back soon."

As she walked away from the table, Holt stared at her for a few moments. She was a hard woman to take your eyes off of. After a minute, she looked back at him, noticing his eyes were still on her. She smiled and waved her fingers at him. Holt rubbed his face and looked away. He felt badly for even looking at her. He thought about Denise.

Hana went into the narrow hallway that led to the bathroom. There was no one else there at the moment. She passed the door to the kitchen. She took a quick look around, and pushed the kitchen door open. There was a pile of boxes to the side of it as she stepped inside the room. She lifted up the box with the empty bottles. Then she started rooting through the next box. There were more empty bottles, and packing material. But buried underneath it were two Glock pistols. Hana smiled.

She took another look around and held them close to her, hiding them with her arms as much as possible. She looked out the small window on the door. The coast was clear. She opened the door and quickly made her way to the bathroom. The door to the bathroom opened and Hana immediately hunched over, as if she were about to be sick.

Once she was inside, and whoever else was in the bathroom left, Hana made her way into a stall. Then, she lifted up her dress and strapped the guns to the inside of her legs, one on each side. She had on a strap on each leg to hold the gun in place. Once the guns were secured, she put her dress back down and left the bathroom.

Hana walked back over to the table, where Holt was still sitting, patiently waiting. She smiled at him.

"We're good to go."

Holt looked her up and down. "Where are they?"

Her smile grew wider. "Wouldn't you like to know?"

His eyes moved toward the slit in her dress.

"When you reach for it, be careful what you grab. Or maybe not."

"When I reach for it?" Holt said. "What exactly do you have in mind?"

"Just follow my lead."

"I'm not sure I like doing that."

"If you have another strategy, I'm all ears."

Holt sighed as he looked around. "No."

Hana stuck out her hand. "Then I guess we should be going. Right? Honey?"

Holt cleared his throat, then reluctantly took her hand as he stood up. They started walking toward the guard on the door.

"Do you have any other strategies you'd like to tell me about once we get up there?"

Hana shrugged. "I was just planning on killing whoever got in our way."

Holt bobbed his head. "Works for me."

27

Holt and Hana approached the door, the guard curiously looking at them. They each handed the man their tickets. He looked them over, then directed them to the wall so they could scan their ID's. Once the light turned green, he opened the door for them.

They walked together up the steps, the stairway dimly lit. They passed a couple coming back down. They couldn't hear anything. It was quiet. Each step brought them closer to their targets, and the weight of their mission settled heavily on their shoulders.

Reaching the second floor landing, they found themselves in a narrow hallway lined with marked doors. Each one had a number on it. The number on their ticket was 6. Odd numbers were to the left. Even numbers to the right. But now, the quiet had evaporated. They could suddenly hear the loud music playing and muffled voices of people inside the rooms.

"Should we take a look?" Hana playfully asked.

"Let's do what we're here for."

They went down to the end of the hallway, where there was an opening to turn left. There was another door down that way. Just one. And there were two men guarding the door. They took a quick peek, making sure they weren't seen. People came out of one of the other rooms, and Hana quickly put her arms around Holt's neck and pulled him close to her, pinning her against the wall. She buried his face into the side of her neck, and she rubbed his back, making sure to make a few moaning noises as well.

"Play the part," she whispered.

Hana kept her eyes peeled and watched the other people in the hallway until they disappeared. Holt and Hana disengaged from each other for the moment as they figured out their next step.

"Let's just shoot them," Hana said.

"Unless you got silencers on those pistols, people are going to hear the shots. We lose the element of surprise before we even get into that room."

"You got a plan?"

Holt glanced at her, uncomfortable at being so close to her. And even faking being intimate. But it was the best way. He took a deep breath before he mentioned what he was thinking.

The Nobody Man

"We turn the corner and go at it hot and heavy until we bring the guards over."

Hana smiled. "I like your thinking."

"They're not gonna want people doing it there in front of them. They'll come over and break us up."

"And when they do… we'll take them out."

"Any objections?"

"Oh, no objections on my end."

"Ready?"

"I've been ready for twenty-four hours."

Holt took a gulp, then grabbed Hana's hand. They quickly strolled into the open part of the hallway and turned left. They didn't even bother looking at the guard's. She pinned him against the wall this time, and they started kissing. Holt felt as guilty as ever. Hana was a beautiful woman, but he wasn't enjoying this at all. His heart was still elsewhere.

"Put your hand inside my dress," Hana whispered. Holt slid his hand against her leg. "Don't be afraid to explore while you're there."

Holt continued feeling her leg until he felt the cold steel he was searching for. He unstrapped the gun from her leg and held it in his hand. The guards watched them for a moment, then looked at each other. Once it seemed like Holt and Hana weren't going to move on their own, the guards started moving towards them.

"They're coming," Holt whispered.

Holt and Hana continued rubbing their free hands

all over each other, kissing each other until the guards got near them.

"Hey, you guys have to move!" one of the guards stated.

Holt and Hana pretended not to hear them.

"I'll follow your lead," Hana said in his ear.

The guards continued getting closer. Then one of them put their hands on Hana to pull her off. As they did, Holt sprung up, pistol in hand, hitting the guard nearest to him in the face with it. He instantly went down. The other guard was stunned for a moment at what he was seeing. As he was about to lunge at Holt, Hana smacked him in the back of the head with her pistol. Both guards were down, barely moving.

Holt immediately grabbed his ID and went over to the door and scanned it. It turned red.

"C'mon!" He tried to scan it again, but it was the same result. "Damn!"

Hana scurried over to him, another badge in hand. "Here. Try this one. It's one of theirs."

Holt took the badge and scanned it. Green. Without hesitation, he put his hand on the door and threw it open. He rushed inside, Hana right behind him, their guns raised high. There were four guards stationed in the room. They were all equally spread out, their backs against the wall, their hands in front of them. They weren't ready for a fight.

Inside the room was an oval table that could seat up to eight comfortably. On this occasion, there were only the three. Kwon and the other two leaders of The Black Phoenix. Upon going into the room, Holt quickly picked out his first target, the man closest to him on the left.

Holt fired, and the man went down. He then set his sights on the next guard. A second later, he was down as well. Hana burst into the room after him, immediately taking the right side of the room. Though the guards on that side were able to get to their pistols, they weren't able to use them. Before they were able to get shots off, they were both eliminated.

Two men at the table jumped up, pulling guns from inside their suit jackets, ready to fire upon the intruders. One of them actually got a shot off. It narrowly missed Hana. She wasn't unnerved, though. She returned fire, putting her man down with one in the chest. Holt did the same.

Holt and Hana both moved closer, one on each side of the table, to Kwon. He was just sitting there calmly, his hands not moving from the table. He didn't seem the least bit affected by what just happened. His four guards, and two associates, taken out in less than a minute. And he sat there with a stoic expression. If one didn't know better, they might have thought he was still in charge. Or held an ace up his sleeve.

"Let's kill him and get out of here," Hana said.

"Not yet. I need some answers first."

"There's no time for that. More will be coming."

"Then give me time," Holt said. "Go over to the door and watch."

Hana sighed, still not thinking it was a good idea. But she was willing to give him the time he was asking. At least for now. If it started to get hot and heavy, all bets were off. Holt pointed his pistol at Kwon's head.

"Who sent you?" Holt asked, a touch of anger in his voice.

Kwon remained quite calm. "I do not even know who you are."

Holt moved in closer. The anger in his voice intensified. "You know exactly who I am. You know what you did. And you know why I'm here."

Kwon continued to stare ahead. "I'm afraid I do not."

"Look at me. Or I'm gonna put a bullet right through your forehead."

Kwon finally moved his eyes and looked at him, and also slightly turned his head towards him.

"Who? And why?"

Kwon gulped. "The why is easy. It was a job. Nothing more."

"Who was the target?"

"You already know the answer to that. You're still here."

"Why? Why would someone want to kill her?"

"Those discussions were never brought up."

Hana had the door slightly open, looking out and waiting for anyone else to appear. She briefly looked back at Holt, feeling some compassion for what he was going through. She hoped he'd get the answers he wanted before they had to go.

"Who hired you?" Holt asked.

"I'm afraid I do not know."

Holt snapped, and immediately hit Kwon on the side of his face with the gun. Kwon was instantly cut open. Holt made sure he didn't hit him so hard to knock him out. He still wanted answers.

"How long do you wanna do this?"

A smile crept onto Kwon's face. "I can do this all day."

"I really don't think you can."

"What do you think this is accomplishing? It won't bring your wife back."

"I just wanna know why."

"You should know. In this business, things are not always as they appear."

"That tells me nothing," Holt said. "Who hired you?"

"We weren't... hired."

"Either you can tell me, or I'll move on to your friends. One of them will talk."

"Please. The other three aren't going to tell you anything either."

Suddenly, gunshots rang out. Hana found a couple of new targets to shoot at. Several more guards had come into the area.

"Aaron, we gotta go!" she yelled between shots.

"Not yet," Holt replied.

"We can't hold them off forever! We don't have enough ammo for that! This was just supposed to be taking them out and then getting out. Not this!"

He quickly glared at her. "Just hold them off."

Hana grunted, but fired a couple more rounds at the guards in the hallway.

"What do you mean you weren't hired?" Holt asked. "Then what was this about?"

Kwon took a deep breath. "It was a personal matter. That's all I can say."

"Personal? To who?"

"Aaron, I don't have enough ammo for this!" Hana yelled.

"Personal to who?!" Holt angrily said.

Another shot rang out. This one had Kwon's name on it. The bullet went right through his forehead, the force of the blast knocking him back in his chair. Holt turned his head and looked at Hana, who still had her gun pointed at the dead man.

"We don't have time," she calmly repeated. "If we don't get out now, we're not getting out."

Holt tried not to let the anger overtake him. He knew Hana was probably correct. But he felt like he was so close to getting an answer. A real answer. He glanced again at Kwon, knowing he wasn't going to get it. At least not from him. Maybe the others still on his list could provide one. But it was hard not to think that he might have just lost his best chance at finding out the truth.

28

Holt and Hana stood there, staring at each other. It was almost as if neither of them were sure whether they should point their guns at the other. But finally, Holt broke his stare and started walking toward her.

"How much you got left?"

Hana quickly checked. "Six shots."

"How many's out there?"

"Three or four."

Holt looked back in the room to see if there was another exit. There was just the window. He went back over to it and looked down. There was a dumpster right below them. He made a face. It wasn't the cleanest of getaways. And it wouldn't be the first time he wound up in the trash. But it sure beat getting into a shootout in the hallway.

"Close the door," Holt said. "Barricade it."

As Hana closed the door and started moving furniture around, Holt fired three rounds into the window. It partially broke, though it was mostly just cracks in the glass. Holt then took a chair and smashed it into the window, breaking off a significant piece of it. He then used his gun to clear off any remaining pieces of glass so they didn't get cut as they jumped through it.

Once Hana was finished with the barricade, she went over to the newly opened window and looked down.

"Seriously?"

Holt shrugged. "Would you rather go the other direction?"

Hana moved her arm up and down, as if she were pointing to her body. "I mean, seriously? In this dress? Do you know how much this cost?"

"I guess you can take your chances going through the hallway."

She rolled her eyes and took another look at the dumpster. "And it's filled with trash. We're gonna stink."

"Softer landing."

Hana sighed. "Fine."

Holt led the way, jumping out as bullets ripped through the door. Hana took one last look, then followed him. She partially landed on Holt, who tried to catch her fall to make it an easier landing for her. They rolled over, with Hana on top of him.

"This wasn't quite the intimate location I had in mind for this."

"Let's go before they find us," Holt replied.

They quickly stood up and climbed out of the dumpster. They started running for their respective cars. Just as they split up, they heard gunfire. A bullet grazed the ground near them.

"Come with me!" Hana said.

They ran in the opposite direction, where her car was parked. She had anticipated this. Within a few minutes, they had gotten to her car and jumped in. She quickly put the car in drive and got out on the road, with bullets striking the back of it as it sped off. Once they were a safe distance away, Hana laughed.

"We pulled it off!"

Holt wasn't quite in the mood to celebrate. All he could think about was the answers he wasn't getting from Kwon anymore. If only he had a little more time. She could see he didn't look happy.

"Hey, you're not still upset about me killing Kwon, are you? I mean, I had to do it."

Holt sighed. "Yeah."

"Look, I know what this means to you, and if it was me, I'd probably do the same. But we just couldn't wait for answers."

"Probably so."

"So what now? Come back to my hotel for that nightcap?"

"Uh, no. I guess just drive around for a little bit until we can get back to my car."

"Why the rush to go back to it?"

"Well, I got a bag in there, and I have to be somewhere else."

"Hong Kong, maybe?"

Holt stared at her. "Maybe."

"I get it."

They drove around for about thirty minutes, eventually getting close enough to drop him off, though it was still a block away. They pulled over to the side of the road.

"Want me to wait around, make sure you're OK?"

"I think I'll be fine," Holt answered.

"It was nice working with you on this. Wish we could've worked even closer."

"Maybe another day."

Hana grinned. "Maybe. I'd like that. I guess I'll see you around."

"Take it easy, huh?"

Holt got out of the car and started walking towards his, staying close to buildings, and out of open spaces or light where he could be seen. With his car in sight, he quickly walked over to it, mindful of any problems along the way. With it being clear, he hopped in, and immediately drove out of the area.

He drove back to the spot where Hana had dropped him off. He parked and took out his phone to call Johnston. She'd been waiting for this and answered right away.

"Hey, you OK?" she hurriedly asked.

"Yeah, I'm good. It's done."

"You got all of them?"

"Well, Kwon and his two associates. Four or five of the guards. A couple of them were left, I think."

"Shouldn't be an issue."

"I'll be on my way to the airport now."

"Um, about that."

Holt didn't like the sound of that and braced himself for bad news. "What's wrong?"

"You won't need to go to Hong Kong now. Or Tokyo either, for that matter."

"Why not?"

"The other two are gone."

Holt hung his head. "I was afraid of that. Just needed to get them all in the same space instead of taking them out one at a time."

"It's not quite that."

"Any idea where they're headed? Maybe I can still track them down."

"Aaron, it's not that. They're already gone."

"Yeah, but I'm not just gonna give up. It might make it more challenging, but it's all I got left."

"I don't mean gone as in left. I mean gone as in dead."

The words stunned him. "What?"

"The two remaining council members of The Black Phoenix are dead."

"Are you sure?"

"We got word about an hour ago. And it was just confirmed about five minutes ago. They're both dead."

"Maybe it's some type of trick."

"It's not. We've got visual evidence. The police are also on the scenes in their respective locations."

"Dead? How can that be?"

"I don't know."

"I mean, that's not a coincidence," Holt said. "Nobody knows anything about these guys for years, and then as soon as I get close, they're found dead?"

"It's definitely suspicious."

"How were they killed?"

"The guy in Hong Kong had his throat cut. The guy in Tokyo was shot in the forehead."

"The forehead." Holt's mind thought back to Kwon, and how Hana shot him in the forehead. Maybe it was a coincidence. "How long have they been dead?"

"Preliminary reports indicate a day or two."

Holt's mind was racing, unsure of what was happening. Everything seemed to be spinning. He wasn't sure how any of this fit together. Florakis, Hana, The Black Phoenix, himself... how did any of it make sense? He was quiet for a minute or two, getting lost in his own thoughts. Johnston kept talking, but she could tell he was somewhere else.

"Aaron? Are you there?"

"Hmm?"

"What's going on?"

"Wish I knew," Holt replied.

"Just so you know, there's various strike teams located all over, ready to take out the remaining members of The Black Phoenix. They're just waiting for the word to go."

"When?"

"Over the next couple days. Looks like this is basically over."

"No, it's not. There's still the guy that killed my wife. And the person that hired him to do it." His mind once again returned to Kwon. "Hired."

"What?"

"Before he was killed, Kwon told me they weren't hired. That it was personal."

"Huh. That's strange. What do you think it means?"

"They weren't hired. It was personal. They did it as a favor for someone."

"But who?"

"I don't know. Has to be someone who…"

Holt's thought trailed off as he thought of the possibilities. But there was one name that kept coming back to him. Florakis. He was the one person who was all over this thing. With Pelligrini. With The Black Phoenix. With him. He seemed to know it all. There was something else bugging him. He couldn't put his

The Nobody Man

finger on what it was yet. But something was there that he wasn't seeing yet.

Holt replayed the entire scenario with Florakis. Then he thought about everything that happened with Kwon. Every moment, every word, every breath. Something was there. Then, as his conversation with Kwon rolled around in his mind, it finally hit him.

"That's it."

"What's it?" Johnston asked.

"We were under the assumption there were five leaders in The Black Phoenix."

"Right. That's what Florakis told us."

"But that's not right. There's six."

"Six? How do you know?"

"When I was talking to Kwon, he said 'the other three aren't going to tell you anything either'. Three. Not two. There were three others. There's another guy in play here."

Johnston thought for a moment. "Florakis."

"He orchestrated this whole thing."

"But why? If he's in bed with them, and he wanted out, why not just kill them himself?"

"Maybe he couldn't. Or maybe he wasn't sure he could succeed. That's why he hired Hana. To make sure the job would be finished."

"Still doesn't make sense to me. He had your wife killed, just to bring you back so you'd kill off his partners?"

Holt scratched the top of his head. "I don't know. Maybe he really did have a problem with me."

"Then why not kill you when you went to his flower shop?"

Holt shook his head. He had a lot of theories. Not many concrete answers.

"I don't know. Maybe it's all connected somehow. Either way, I gotta get back to that flower shop."

"Head back to the airport. I'll have the plane take a detour."

Holt hung up and immediately drove to the airport. There was a private plane waiting there for him. Once he got out of his car, he grabbed his bag, and double-checked his pockets. He felt something. It felt like a piece of paper in his back pocket. He took it out. It was folded up into a square. He unfolded it and read it.

"Aaron, by the time you read this you'll probably know there's nothing left for you in Hong Kong or Tokyo. Yes, it was me. I'm sure you wanted to finish this up yourself. Sorry, it's not personal. It was just a job. I did those before I even met you or knew your circumstances. I'm not sure of why on any of the details. It's just what I was hired to do. Wherever you're headed next, I hope you find whatever peace you're looking for. And I'd still really like to get that nightcap sometime. Hana."

A small hint of a smile formed on the corner of Holt's lips. "I wonder where she was keeping this all that time?"

The Nobody Man

He then thought back to the dumpster. She probably slipped it into his pocket while they were in there. Or maybe it was while they were in the hallway making out. It didn't really matter when. If she was to be trusted, and believed, she wasn't involved in anything other than being hired to do a job. He took a little comfort in that. He would have hated it if he discovered she was involved somehow and had to kill her.

He put her out of his mind. Now, Holt's mind turned to Florakis. He was the key to everything. And there was no doubt in Holt's mind that Florakis knew a lot more than he said the last time they spoke. Maybe he was even the one behind everything. Holt didn't know. But he was damn sure going to find out.

29

By the time Holt arrived back in Greece, it was already the following morning. It was a long flight, and a six-hour time difference. He wasted no time in heading straight for the flower shop. He waited across the street for a while, just keeping an eye out for anyone going in or out of the store. But after sitting there for close to an hour, nobody did.

Finally tired of waiting, Holt figured he'd press the issue. He walked across the street and entered the flower shop. The bell above the door jingled as he stepped inside. He put his hand on his gun, though he didn't pull it out yet, ready for anything. He quickly scanned the room, looking for Florakis. There was no one to be found.

He thought it strange that the door was open, but nobody was at home. He remembered the back office the last time he was there. First, Holt casually strolled around the room, making sure no one was hiding anywhere. Behind the counter, or maybe a secret compartment somewhere.

Once he was satisfied he was not in store for a surprise, Holt walked to the back room. The door to the office was closed. Holt stood beside it, took a deep breath, and removed his gun. After a second, he put his hand on the door and quickly pushed it open.

Still not giving anyone inside a target to shoot at, he bobbed his head several times to look in there. It appeared empty, though. He finally stepped inside, though it didn't take long to see nobody was there.

It was very strange. Unless Florakis left in such a hurry that he didn't even care about locking up, which was always possible. Still, Holt couldn't shake the feeling that something else was going on here. He just didn't know what yet.

He started looking around, sitting behind the desk and going onto the desktop computer on it. Maybe there was some clue on there that would tell him what Florakis was up to or where he was going. After ten minutes, though, he wasn't having much luck. There didn't seem to be anything on there other than flower shop business.

Then, he heard the bell ring over the door to enter. Holt slowly got up, grabbing his gun, as he left the office. He walked over to the swinging door that separated the main room from the back. There was a small window in the center of it, and he looked through it, but didn't see anyone out there. Of course, from that view, he couldn't see the entire shop. Anyone standing to the far left of him was blocked from his view.

Holt slowly pushed the door open, and took a peek around the door.

"Hey, what's the word?" a man asked. "Hear anything yet?"

Holt fully stepped out into the room, seeing a man sitting next to the counter. The man had his phone out, his head buried and looking at something on it. Holt could hardly believe his eyes, though. It was the man that killed his wife. He didn't have the red hat on, but Holt would know that face anywhere. It flashed in his mind often enough.

Holt's body filled with emotions. But one overtook him more than any other. And that was rage. He holstered his gun and started running at the man, who was still on his phone. It wasn't until Holt was almost on top of him that he noticed what was going on. He instantly dropped his phone and reached for his gun, but not until Holt took a flying leap and knocked him off the chair. The man's gun also dropped to the floor.

Holt immediately got on top of the guy and started pounding away at his face. This is what Holt had been hoping for. Sure, he could've just taken the shot and ended it quickly, but that wasn't really what Holt wanted. He wanted this guy to pay. He wanted him to feel pain before he ended it. He wanted the man to see it coming first. He wanted him to worry, to beg, to have

The Nobody Man

that impending sense of doom that would overtake his body when he saw his life flashing before his eyes.

The man was a skilled fighter in his own right, though. And he fought back. Though Holt had the upper hand, the man was able to shove him off, and return a few punches. They both got in a few licks, and for a few moments, it looked like it might have been an even contest. But only for a few moments. It wasn't long before Holt once again proved to be the better fight. He even grabbed a flower pot and smashed it over the man's face. The pot exploded into chunks of tiny pieces as the man hit the floor.

Holt stood over him, the rage still coursing through his veins. He couldn't control himself, and continued wailing on the man's face, a barrage of punches easily flowing from his fists. The man on the ground was barely conscious at this point and wasn't even able to fight back or defend himself. Holt continued punching the man within an inch of his life.

But then he stopped. As if someone had tapped him on the shoulder and told him that was enough. Holt looked wide-eyed at the man, wanting to finish him off. But he suddenly stood up for some reason.

"Who hired you?" Holt asked. He believed he already knew the answer, Theo Florakis, but he wanted to hear it confirmed.

The man rolled over, spitting up blood, which mixed with the blood that was streaming down his face from multiple cuts. He started crawling on his hands and knees. He noticed his gun lying on the ground a few feet away. Holt noticed it too. But he wasn't going to stop the man from reaching for it. Not yet.

Holt turned his back on the man and walked a few steps in the other direction. He went to the window and looked out. It was a beautiful day. Warm. Sunny. A small crowd of people walking up and down the street. A stark contrast from what was going on inside that flower shop.

Then, Holt heard a noise from behind. It sounded like the man was scurrying towards his gun on the floor. Holt instantly turned around, seeing the man put his fingers on the weapon. Holt fired three rounds, each one hitting the man in the chest. His adversary was gone immediately.

Holt stood there, staring at the dead body, hoping something would change within him. Like a weight would be lifted off his shoulders. Or his mind would suddenly become clear. But it was nothing like that. He didn't feel any different at all. He still felt the rage. Nothing would change that at this point.

He then saw the man's phone on the floor. Holt went over to it and picked it up. It was password-protected. Hacking into things wasn't his specialty. But maybe they could find something inside that would lead to where Florakis had gone. He put the phone in his pocket and left the flower shop, locking the door behind him.

Once outside, Holt took a quick look around to make sure he wasn't being watched. The crowd was sparse at the moment. He walked away from the store, taking out his own phone to call Johnston.

"Hey, how's Greece? Any progress?"

"I guess you could say that," Holt answered.

"Did you find Florakis?"

"Nah. He's gone. I found something else unexpected, though. I found the guy in the red hat."

Johnston was almost dumbfounded. "What?"

"He walked into the flower shop. Sat down. Didn't even seem to know I was there."

"Oh, wow. So what happened?"

"There's a mess in the flower shop."

She didn't need to know the details to know the result. "Um, OK. Wow. So that is unexpected. What do you make of it?"

"He walked in and said something. Something about whether he'd heard anything. I assume it was to Florakis. Seems like maybe they were working together."

"So Florakis hired him to... you know."

"Seems like."

"So what's your next move?"

"I dunno. Doesn't seem like I have one right now. Florakis is gone. And unless you can tell me where he went, right now I got nothing."

"I can get on it."

"In the meantime, I've got the man's phone. The

guy with the red hat. Didn't figure he'd need it anymore. Thought maybe it could give us some insight into where Florakis might be."

"That's good. What's on it?"

"Don't know," Holt replied. "Can't get in it. Figured you might have better luck with it."

"OK. Why don't you come back here and I'll take it, see what I can come up with."

Holt sighed, not really wanting to go back home. It felt like taking a step backward.

"Look, I know you want to stay out there, hunting around, but right now, we don't have anything. It doesn't mean we have to give up. It's just taking a brief pause until we get a better line on him, that's all. So come back, I'll take the phone, and we'll get working on it."

Holt closed his eyes for a moment. "OK. I'll be on the next flight out."

"Sounds good. I'll see you soon."

Holt hung up, and took a deep breath. The man that ordered his wife's death was still out there. But at least he got the man that was sent to carry it out. It was at least one thing off his plate. Though it didn't feel like any weight was lifted off his shoulders, at least it was one less thing on his mind. If it was anything, it was a small victory. At least he had that.

30

One week later – Johnston was scrambling inside her apartment, trying to get ready. She had a meeting with Holt along the Potomac River. But she couldn't find her keys at the moment. Then, there was a knock at the door. It was odd. She wasn't expecting anyone. Maybe Holt decided to surprise her and save her the trip, though she never told him her address. A man like Holt was resourceful, though, so it wouldn't have surprised her if he found out somehow.

She hurried to the door and opened it, half-expecting it to be Holt. The pleasant face she had quickly evaporated and she let out a sigh.

"Jared. What are you doing here?"

"Can I come in?"

She knew it was against her better judgment, and she let out a small groan, but stepped back and extended her arms.

"I suppose."

He walked in and looked around. He noticed she had her shoes on. "Going somewhere?"

"Uh, yeah, actually. I have a meeting in a few minutes, so this can't take long."

Jared looked at his watch. "A meeting now? It's after seven."

Johnston shrugged. "What can I tell you? In my world, things don't always happen between nine and five. So why are you here?"

Jared rubbed his hands together. "I'm leaving in the morning."

She tried to put on a smile. "Well, good luck."

"I still would like you to come. I mean, not right away obviously. I know you'd have to get things squared away here first. But..."

"There's no but's. I'm not coming. I thought I made that plainly evident to you already."

"Jo, I really just want to be able to figure this out. I love you."

Johnston licked her lips and closed her eyes, not really wanting to deal with this again. "Jared, there's nothing more to say. I'm not leaving here. This is where I belong right now. We have two different goals right now. And that's fine. People, even couples, are allowed to want different things for their lives. And that's where we're at right now."

Jared sighed and took a step toward her, trying to

put his hand on her waist. Johnston took a step back, preventing him from doing so.

"No, no. No. We're done. There's nothing else to say. Nothing else to talk about. We don't have to separate as enemies or under bad terms. We can still be friends. And who knows what the future holds? But right now, I think our future doesn't include *us*. So let's just leave it at that and walk away with us both having good memories together."

Jared lowered his head. "So that's really your final answer, huh?"

"Yeah. It is."

Jared slowly walked past her. "All right, then." He opened the door and looked back. "I guess I'll see you when I see you."

Johnston nodded. "Good luck with the job. I know you'll do great."

As Jared walked away, Johnston closed the door. She took a deep breath, then started looking for her keys again. She finally found them underneath some mail on the kitchen counter. She took another deep breath and closed her eyes again. She then went to a full-size mirror in her bedroom.

"OK. It's only two years of your life. No big deal, right?" She fixed her hair a little and sighed. "Right."

She then left her apartment and drove to the river. She was to meet Holt at the Rock Creek Trail, not far from the John F. Kennedy Center for the Performing

Arts. By the time she got there, saw Holt leaning on the railing, overlooking the river. He turned his head, noticing her walking towards him. He didn't move as she took the spot next to him. She looked out at the water.

"It's always beautiful here. Calming."

Holt looked at the water, and briefly at the sky. "Yeah."

"So we're still working on the phone. So far, haven't come up with much. But you know, we're not giving up."

Holt lowered his head, disappointed by the news, though it wasn't unexpected. He assumed as much since she hadn't contacted him sooner.

"What about Florakis?"

She took a deep breath, which was really all Holt needed to hear to know what was coming next.

"No sign of him at this point. But again... still looking. He'll turn up at some point."

"Dig into his background more?"

"We have. Still don't know his connection to all this yet. There's nothing we can find so far that ties the two of you together."

"He's good at hiding his tracks, apparently."

"Oh, so you know, The Black Phoenix is officially disbanded."

"Thought that was official after Singapore?"

"Well, you took care of the leadership. We took care of the rest. The coordinated strikes were a success. Every agent on that list is accounted for."

"Any still alive?"

"No."

"So how do we know that's all of them?" Holt asked. "Because Florakis said so? He's obviously got ulterior motives. Maybe he's got his own stash of agents."

"I guess we can't rule anything out at this time. But so far, there's nothing that indicates that's the case. But we'll keep an eye out."

"Somebody out there knows something. And I'm gonna find them."

"What do you really think this was all about? I mean, it started with you. But it turned into a lot more. Was it just to lure you back into doing this?"

Holt shook his head. "I don't think so. I think it started as something personal. Still is. Florakis used his ties to Black Phoenix to hunt me down. Took years to do so. He wanted Denise dead and for me to feel that pain, for whatever reason. Knowing my relationship with Pelligrini, he knew I'd eventually come knocking. Maybe in addition to whatever I did to him before, he wanted out of The Black Phoenix. From all we can tell, once you're in, you don't get out. Maybe he figured he could hurt me, and help himself at the same time."

"So he gave you the names of everyone in the organization, where you could find them, and then just turned you loose?"

"If I succeed, he goes free. If I lose, nobody on the

inside suspects him. I'm just a deranged lunatic looking for revenge."

"Where does Hana fit in?"

Holt shrugged. "Making sure the job got finished. He knew she could do the other two jobs alone. The White Horse Lounge would take the both of us. And when that was finished, he knew I'd go back to Greece to look for him."

"And in knowing that, he brings the other guy in for a meeting, knowing you'll be there waiting for him at the same time."

"All the loose ends are tied off. There's nothing that connects anyone to Florakis now."

"That's where you're wrong," Johnston said. "There is someone. Hana."

"Who you also can't find."

Johnston briefly put her hand on his forearm. "But we're not stopping. We're not giving up. Something will turn up. Somewhere. At some time. And when we do, we'll pounce."

"Yeah. However long that may be."

Johnston touched his arm. "Hey, don't be discouraged. This isn't the end. I promise. You can trust me."

Holt turned and faced her, a slight smile forming. "I already do."

He started to walk past her, though she gently grabbed his arm again. "Where are you going?"

"I have a grave to visit."

Johnston let go of him and smiled.

"Thanks for not pressing," Holt said.

"On?"

"Bringing me back."

"Oh. Yeah, well, it's not the right time for you. Maybe another time."

Holt stuck his hand out, and they shook hands.

"Thank you. For helping."

Johnston fought back the tears from forming in her eyes. "Of course."

"Well, when you find something, you know where to find me."

"I do. And I will."

Holt then took a few steps back and walked away. Johnston stood there, watching him leave. Her phone rang. She looked at the ID. It was Barnes.

"How'd your meeting go?"

"Good," Johnston replied.

"Is he back in the fold?"

She hesitated. "Not yet. But I'm confident. He'll be back."

"How sure are you?"

"Almost a hundred percent. I almost guarantee it. We'll see him again."

ALSO BY MIKE RYAN

Continue reading The Aaron Holt Series with the next book in the series, Out Of The Shadows.

Other Books:

The Silencer Series

The Nate Thrower Series

The Cari Porter Series

The Extractor Series

The Cain Series

The Eliminator Series

The Ghost Series

The Brandon Hall Series

A Dangerous Man

The Last Job

The Crew

ABOUT THE AUTHOR

Mike Ryan is a USA Today Bestselling Author. He lives in Pennsylvania with his wife, and four children. He's the author of the bestselling Silencer Series, as well as many others. Visit his website at www.mikeryanbooks.com to find out more about his books, and sign up for his newsletter. You can also interact with Mike via Facebook, and Instagram.

www.ingramcontent.com/pod-product-compliance
Ingram Content Group UK Ltd.
Pitfield, Milton Keynes, MK11 3LW, UK
UKHW020902020425
5252UKWH00061B/452